by nancy thayer

let it snow

let it snow

A Novel

nancy
thayer

BALLANTINE BOOKS
NEW YORK

Copyright © 2019 by Nancy Thayer

Published in the United States by Ballantine Books,
an imprint of Random House, a division of
Penguin Random House LLC, New York.

BALLANTINE and the HOUSE colophon are registered trademarks
of Penguin Random House LLC.

Hardback ISBN 9781524798680
Ebook ISBN 9781524798697

Printed in the United States of America on acid-free paper

randomhousebooks.com

2 4 6 8 9 7 5 3 1

First Edition

Book design by Susan Turner

This book is for

Ellias

&

Adeline F¹⁰

&

Emmett

&

Anathea

acknowledgments

When I started writing *Let It Snow,* the first sentence flew onto the page exactly as it is now. It was as if I was watching real people, and I knew their names at once.

Wink. I know two people on Nantucket named Wink. One is a beautiful young woman. The other is a charming older man. Neither one is a nine-year-old girl. *My* Wink showed up on the page entirely and completely herself, and she brought the novel with her.

I've always wanted to use the name Christina, after the gorgeous woman with the tumbling dark hair who works in a shop on Nantucket. Actually, I wanted to use her first and last names, but that could get tricky. But *my* Christina also appeared as magically as Wink, and I just hitched onto them and let them take me into the story.

Okay, it wasn't all magical. I truly could not have written this book without the help, suggestions, and advice from my brilliant editor, Shauna Summers, and from the ever-quick-witted Meg Ruley and Christina Hogrebe. Now that I think about it, maybe it *was* magical, because those three women knew exactly what was needed and what to do. Thank you, Shauna, Meg, and Christina.

I realize every day how fortunate I am to be with the Ballantine team. Gina Centrello, Kara Welsh, and Kim Hovey, I send you pots of gratitude. Lexi Batsides, you have always been so helpful, and so quick! Thank you. Allison Schuster and Karen Fink, you've done marvels with the publicity, especially during that stretch of time when I wasn't always conscious or lucid. Really, you two are champions.

I've been fortunate to have Madeline Hopkins as copyeditor. Or is it copy-editor? A friend sent me the most marvelous, witty, and helpful book titled (or is it entitled?) *Dreyer's English,* about the correct use of punctuation and grammar and all the bits and pieces that make a book comprehensible and enjoyable. If you're a writer, buy it. If you like to laugh, buy it. But back to Madeline Hopkins—thank you so sincerely and enormously for your careful work. And Jennifer Rodriguez, thank you. You both made a great difference in this book that I care about so much.

Thanks to Sara Mallion, Chris Mason, Alexandra LaPaglia, and more recently Susan McGinnis (who I'll just quickly mention played Miranda's secretary in *Sex and the City*) for all your help with publicity and general *stuff.*

Jill, Deborah, Martha, Tricia, Janet, Sofiya, Toni, Antonia, Mary, John, and Mark, I prize every moment I get to be with you.

Josh, David, Sam, Tommy, Ellias, Adeline, Emmett, and Annie, you guys are just WOW!

And my husband, Charley—what a miracle that we found each other. In the evenings, when we sit in our comfortable, slightly sagging armchairs, each reading a book while our cat Callie purrs next to Charley, it is heaven.

Finally, I hope my Facebook readers know how precious they are to me. They brighten my life and make my world larger, and more beautiful. Thank you all.

let it snow

1

Christina Antonioni could spot a shoplifter with her eyes blindfolded and both ears stuffed with cotton. You didn't run a toy shop for five years without developing a certain intuition. Right now her own private alarm system was pinging all over her body.

The girl was about nine years old, a cute child with messy blond hair falling into her shifty blue eyes. On this cold early December day, she wore sneakers, jeans, and a shapeless wool sweater.

"Merry Christmas!" Christina greeted her with a smile.

"Merry Christmas," the girl mumbled sullenly. She didn't look at Christina. With her thin shoulders hunched, she slunk around the little shop, casting a brooding glance at the wooden ferry replicas, lighthouses, books, fairies, and mermaids.

She paused at the mermaid book. Christina knew she would. She knew what girls her age liked. The most fabulous item there, a huge embossed book about mermaids with a faux jewel glittering in the middle, was too big for the girl to steal, and so was the ten-inch, beautifully made mermaid doll on a nearby shelf.

Christina bent down to put something in her glass display case. Through the glass she saw the girl swiftly slide a small mermaid sticker book into the pocket of her jeans.

It was only a five-dollar item. She wanted to let her have it, poor child.

But children should be taught not to steal.

"Please put the sticker book back," Christina ordered in a firm voice.

The girl jumped. She glared at Christina with her mouth bunched up in defiance. Then, to Christina's chagrin, her face turned red and she burst into tears.

"It's not fair!" she wailed. "I only took a little thing."

"It's still stealing," she quietly reminded the child.

"It's Christmas!" the girl blubbered. "My parents are getting divorced, and my mom and I are staying with my grandfather and I don't have any toys or dolls here and we don't even have a Christmas tree! I just want *something*!"

"Oh, honey." Christina could tell the girl's grief was genuine. She stepped out from behind the counter, approaching her as if she were a wounded wild animal.

Perhaps the child thought Christina was going to wrench the sticker book away from her. She jerked it from her jeans pocket and threw it toward the shelf. "There!"

"What's your name?" Christina asked gently.

Warily, she muttered, "Wink."

"Wink, thank you for returning the sticker book. I'm sorry to hear about your situation. Tell you what. If you'll come back later today, around three o'clock, I'll give you a job. The UPS man arrives then and you can help carry the boxes into the shop. I'll pay you and you can buy yourself a present here. I'll give you a discount so you can buy something nice."

Wink stared at her as if she'd just grown another head. "What if you have the police here?" Her voice quavered and she flushed at the telltale anxiety in her voice.

"You didn't steal the stickers. You put them back." Something in her wanted to give this girl her dignity. "Wink, this is a serious offer. I need the help."

She chewed on her lip, thinking. "Okay," she agreed. "I'll be back at three."

She sauntered out of the shop, her shoulders just a little bit straighter.

At noon, Christina put a WILL RETURN IN THIRTY MINUTES sign on her door, locked it, and went across the brick avenue to Mimi's Seaside Souvenirs. Mimi Mattes, Jacob Greenwood, and Harriet Colby were already there, gathered in the windowless back room where Mimi had set up folding chairs among the cardboard packing boxes.

They comprised an informal group they called the Shedders because they each rented one of the weathered, shingled sheds on the wharf that extended out over the water.

Their shops were each a single quaint—and *quaint* was a compliment—room. Years ago, fishermen had tied up their boats to this wharf and lugged their catches into the relative shelter of these shingled buildings to clean and dress for sale. Later, the long pier was surfaced with bricks, the sheds were turned into shops, and the Hy-Line ferry arrived, carrying people to and from the mainland several times a day.

Because of the ferry, the little sheds were great places for tourists to browse and find one last Nantucket gift to take home. The bad news was the sheds weren't insulated or centrally heated. There was electricity, of course, and behind their counters the shopkeepers each had a small electric oil-filled heater that made the fiercest winter days tolerable.

Mimi had the biggest shed so the Shedders met there for a quick lunch most days, exchanging gossip and helpful information. The chamber of commerce had a message system to alert merchants of potential shoplifters, and Christina wasn't sure whether to inform them about the girl.

Huddled next to the heater, Christina described her confrontation with the child.

"Poor child," Mimi Mattes sighed. In her fifties, widowed, Mimi was as round and cheerful as a snowwoman, with short, curly white hair and sparkling blue eyes. "You did the right thing, Christina. I don't think we need to send out an alert."

"I agree," Jacob chimed in. He was in his thirties, an odd, handsome, yet somehow dorky guy who ran Nantucket Wind Man. Jacob sold kites, wind chimes, weather vanes, and scientific equipment such as barometers, thermometers, and anemometers. "In fact, I have an idea," he continued. "Let's give the kid a real Christmas. Let's each put a gift in a bag. Christina can surprise her with it at the end of the day. I'll donate a handheld electronic weather gauge."

"Lovely, Jacob!" Mimi clapped her plump, dimpled hands. "I'll give her a Christmas sweatshirt. Sounds like she can use it."

Christina nodded enthusiastically. "You guys are the best. I'll give her the mermaid sticker book she was drooling over."

Three expectant faces turned toward Harriet, who gazed sourly back. Harriet was new to the wharf. She'd come from Connecticut, and one evening when they all went out together for drinks, she confessed she was there to find a wealthy husband. Her shop, Nantucket Couture, was a bit of a joke to those who lived on the island, since the island's *couture* pretty much consisted of a bathing suit and flip-flops. Still, people needed something for the summer parties, and Harriet made a killing then. This season she concentrated on clever gloves, shawls, and caps.

"I don't carry merchandise for *children*," she reminded them, shuddering delicately at the thought of the little savages. Harriet could get away with her attitude because she was gorgeous. Blunt-cut blond hair brushed her shoulders, sea-green eyes slanted like a cat's, and her figure was exceedingly vavoom.

Christina admired Harriet's looks, and some days she envied them; who wouldn't? Still, Christina's own abundant brown curls tumbled romantically down her back; she'd been told she resembled a Pre-Raphaelite heroine. In college, she'd almost gotten engaged to a man she'd dated for a year, but at graduation they decided to go their separate ways. At twenty-five, she'd dated a really good guy, Jamie Locke, but when he proposed to her, she turned him down, as nicely as she could. Christina believed in true love. She was holding out for what she privately called the Big Bang. If the universe could start that way, so could her married life. She wanted to meet The Man and know at once, with a kind of emotional explosion, that he was The One.

Harriet shifted on her chair. "All right. I'll give her some money." She reached into her Prada bag and pulled out a dollar bill. "Here, Christina."

"A dollar?" Christina snorted with laughter. "Don't go wild, Harriet."

"Look, if I gave every pathetic kid a dollar, I'd be bankrupt," Harriet argued.

"I'll tell you what," Christina said. "Give me another dollar. I'll give you a discount on the mermaid sticker book and you can give her that."

Harriet drew back in horror. "Well, I don't want to *see* her!"

"You don't have to interact with her," Christina promised. "I'll tell her it's from you."

"Whatever." Harriet sighed, ferreting around in her bag for another dollar bill.

At three, the UPS truck trundled over the bricks and stopped outside Christina's Toy Shop.

"Hey, there, Christina, how are ya?" Chuck, the driver, jumped down and began to unload boxes.

"Good, Chuck. You?" Christina came out of her shop with a smile for the driver but a sinking heart. Wink hadn't returned.

"Lots of work these days. It's a busy season," Chuck told her, heading for the back of the truck. He slid the panel door up.

A cough caught Christina's attention. She turned to see Wink standing at the corner of her shop, staring down at the bricks, shoulders clenched.

"Wink!" Christina called brightly. "You're here. Thank heavens. Chuck, this is Wink. She's going to help carry in the boxes for me."

"Good for you, kid!" Chuck said. "But you know, I can carry them inside."

"Not today, thanks," Christina said firmly.

"Okay with me. Here, take this one." He handed one of the smaller brown boxes to the girl.

Christina went inside. She showed Wink where to stack the boxes behind the counter.

The girl's face turned red with effort, but she didn't complain, and Christina refused to feel pity, because the merchandise was mostly small objects, and the brown boxes they arrived in were small, too.

After Chuck left, a customer stopped by, so she asked Wink to wait a moment for her pay. The woman bought a miniature wicker picnic basket with child-size plates and utensils strapped neatly in place for her granddaughter and left.

"You worked about fifteen minutes," Christina said to Wink, who was leaning on one of the boxes, looking expectant. "At twenty dollars an hour, that makes your pay one quarter of an hour, which is five dollars." She put a five-dollar bill on the counter next to her.

"*Five* dollars?" The girl's shoulders slumped.

Christina wanted to explain that she hadn't even worked fifteen minutes, and the UPS man would have carried all the boxes into the shop by himself, and in this economy she cherished every five dollars she possessed.

But it was Christmas. "Also, I have a present for you, Wink." She handed her the gift bag.

Or tried to. Wink drew back, as if afraid to touch the bag. "I-I-I don't have anything for you," she stuttered.

"Oh, sweetie, that's all right. Here. Take it. I think you'll like it."

Wink took the bag, peeking down into it as if afraid a snake hid there, coiled to strike. Her eyes widened as she spotted the weather gauge, sweatshirt, and sticker book. She took the sticker book out, setting the bag down so she could hold it with both hands. Her lower lip trembled. Furiously, she blinked back the tears welling in her eyes.

"Awesome," she breathed. "Thank you, um, Miss Christina."

"You are most welcome, Wink. Merry Christmas." *This is what Christmas is all about,* Christina thought. She almost cried, too.

Wink's face brightened even more. "And I can use my five dollars to buy my mom a present!"

"Excellent idea," Christina said.

Wink turned to face Christina, her chin high, her

dignity fully restored. "Miss Christina," she asked, "could I hug you?"

"Miss Wink," Christina replied, "I would like that very much." She crouched to be eye level with the girl.

Wink threw her arms around Christina and squeezed her hard.

Christina swallowed a big gulp of emotion. Someday she would have her own children. Until then, this was one of the sweetest embraces she'd ever known.

Wink released her, grabbed her presents, took the five-dollar bill from the counter, and headed for the door. "Merry Christmas!" she called, and raced away down the wharf, out of sight.

2

"You guys are a pair of suckers," Harriet said, rolling her eyes.

It was the next day. The Shedders were eating lunch again at Mimi's, huddled around the heater. Christina had described giving Wink her gift. Mimi and Jacob were delighted, but Harriet scoffed at their sentimentality.

"She's probably a little scam artist," Harriet continued. "She probably does this at all the shops."

"Don't be such a pessimist," Jacob told her.

Harriet glanced at Jacob and sighed. "I'll try, but it's hard."

Christina changed the subject. "I'm not going to take an entire half hour today. Tomorrow the Christmas Stroll starts. The shoppers are out. Are you guys doing good business?"

Mimi nodded. "The sweatshirts are flying out of here, especially the ones I had made up with Santa riding the back of a whale."

"I'm almost sold out of pinwheels," Jacob reported.

"Pinwheels are hardly going to pay the rent," Harriet reminded him.

"True," Jacob agreed. "But the expensive science stuff is selling, too. Plus, lots of people are taking pamphlets about wind energy."

"Oh, groan," Harriet said. "Can't you stop saving the world for one day? Don't you need to make a buck?"

Mimi smoothly intervened. She stood up, which never failed to get attention, since all two hundred and some pounds of her was clad in her wildly patterned Christmas sweater. "Children," she said sweetly, "no fighting. It's Christmas. I, for one, am going to finish my sandwich at the counter. I can hear people milling about outside."

Christina, Jacob, and Harriet packed up the remainder of their lunches, said goodbye, and braved the frigid December wind as they crossed from Mimi's Seaside Souvenirs to their own shops.

A gaggle of mothers waited outside Christina's shop, stamping their feet to keep warm as the wind off the sea flapped their scarves and mufflers.

Christina threw open the door. "Come in!" she called cheerfully.

Christina never did finish her sandwich. Stroll Weekend, the first weekend in December, brought in crowds.

The mothers bought mermaids, pirates, seagulls, and seals. They bought treasure chests, books, puzzles, and wooden lighthouses. Shrieking with happiness at finding the perfect stocking stuffer, they seized up sticker books, wooden pull-toys, and replicas of the Nantucket Rainbow Fleet sailboats.

Christina rang up sales, tucked gifts into bags, answered questions, pointed directions, and chatted with her customers. At one interlude, she found time to flick on her CD player, filling the air with Christmas carols, and the music gave her the energy to work as fast as she could all afternoon.

It was after five when the crowd thinned out. Christina usually closed at six, but today and tomorrow she'd stay open until no one else arrived.

Night had fallen. Darkness surrounded the wharf, while the winter wind increased, blustering and shoving against the thin walls of the shop, splashing harbor water loudly against the wooden floor. Out here on the wharf you could feel the full force of winter, the depth of the dark. Christina was grateful for the cheer of the Christmas lights outlining the other shops, twinkling companionably in the blackness. Everything would be much more romantic if it would snow. Snow always laced and frosted the windows of homes and shops, turning them all into presents. But no snow yet.

Christina walked around her shop, straightening the shelves, getting ready for the next day. She was just thinking of locking up for the night when a woman entered.

The woman's ears flashed with diamonds beneath her fur hat. She was young, only a bit older than Christina, and very pretty, except for the disdainful expression on her face.

She held up a bag. "Did you give these *things* to my daughter?"

Christina hesitated. She'd never, ever, had a parent

complain before. "I'm not sure," she responded mildly. "Could I see what you have?"

The woman dumped the bag upside down on the counter. Out clattered a sweatshirt, a weather gauge, and the sticker book.

Stunned, Christina protested, "These were gifts for Wink." And Wink, Christina felt certain, didn't have a mother who went around in diamonds.

"I see. Well, that's very sweet of you, but completely unnecessary. I'm returning them. You can give them to some child who needs them."

A man entered the store, a sheepish expression on his handsome face. Like Wink and the angry woman, he had thick blond hair and blue eyes, thickly fringed with brown lashes. "Delia," he said quietly. "Please."

His wife—Christina assumed she was his wife—ignored him. Looking down her nose at Christina, she smiled condescendingly. "You see, my daughter, Winifred Bittlesman Lombard, is the granddaughter of Oscar Bittlesman!"

Even Christina, who paid little attention to such things, knew that Oscar Bittlesman was wealthy. Years ago, he'd been the talk of the town when he had bought a house on the cliff worth ten million dollars, and three years ago, unlike all the other millionaires, he starting living there year-round.

He had also bought the wharf property and all the buildings on it. Christina and the other Shedders were on tenterhooks, waiting to see if the new owner would raise the rent.

"So," Delia continued, "we are more than capable of providing Winifred with plenty of gifts."

"I'm sure you are," Christina began. "I apologize if I somehow insulted you. I didn't know Wink's last name, and she indicated that her family couldn't—" She stopped. She didn't want to get the girl in trouble with this proud woman. "She was sad that her parents are getting divorced," she concluded truthfully.

Wink's mother rolled her eyes and laughed. "Oh, dear. All you people love to gossip about us!"

"What?" Delia Bittlesman Lombard's attitude was getting up Christina's nose. "I really don't think—"

"You don't need to think. Just don't give anything to my daughter again." Tossing her head, elbowing the man in her hurry, she strode from the store, her fur coat sailing out behind her like the wings of a flying squirrel.

"I apologize for my sister," the man said.

Christina blinked as her mind processed this information. So this tall, handsome, and seemingly rational man was not the crazy woman's husband.

"She's not usually like that," the man continued. "The divorce is upsetting for her and she's unsettled, spending Christmas on an island where she knows no one. Stress brings out the worst in her."

Christina kept silent. She didn't want to say, *Oh, that's all right.* She was trembling from the encounter. She neatly folded up the tousled sweatshirt and smoothed the cover of the sticker book.

"Please forgive us," the man said. Coming toward her, he held out his hand. "I'm Andy Bittlesman, by the way."

With a charming smile, he added wryly, "Oscar Bittlesman's son, and I can't do a thing about that."

He'd made her smile. She took his hand. "Christina Antonioni."

"Nice name." He continued to hold her hand in his larger, warmer one.

Was he flirting with her? For all she knew, he was married. Or more likely enjoying a moment of *noblesse oblige*. Throw the peasant a bone and keep her happy.

"How's Wink?" Christina asked, gently sliding her hand away from Andy's.

"She's been better," Andy admitted. "Her parents' divorce is difficult for her. I think it's worse because she's an only child. We thought it would be fun for her to spend Christmas on the island, but we didn't count on the cold. She can't play on the beach or go swimming. There's no snow for a snowman. And she doesn't know any other kids."

"Have you taken her to the library?" Christina suggested. "There's a marvelous children's wing."

"Well, no," Andy said, "we haven't thought of that. I'll tell Delia."

"Tell her about the Whaling Museum, too. It's a fabulous place for kids Wink's age. It's got a real whale skeleton hanging from the ceiling."

"That sounds great. I'd like to see it, too."

"And when the weather's decent," Christina added, caught up in Andy's enthusiastic response, "you can walk up to The Creeks at the end of the harbor. And along the wharves. Dolphins have been spotted there recently."

"Really? Cool." For a moment Andy stood daydreaming.

Lowering his head, he peered up at her from beneath his long lashes. "I don't suppose you'd like to come along, too?"

Christina couldn't help herself—it was a stimulus-response kind of thing—her eyes flew to his left hand. No wedding ring.

"But you're probably busy," Andy continued, suddenly flustered. "Or married. Or at least engaged." He was looking at her ring finger, too.

Christina laughed. "Not married. Not engaged. But overwhelmed. The month of December is crazy busy."

"Oh, well, sure, I understand." Andy cocked his head, studying Christina. "How about in the evenings? Could I take you out to dinner?"

"Oh," Christina protested, suddenly embarrassed. "You don't have to do that."

"I don't *have* to, but I certainly would like to," Andy told her.

"Well . . ." Christina paused. "Don't you have to get back to the city?"

"Not until I've taken you out to dinner, Christina Antonioni," Andy Bittlesman said.

His smile was like an arrow straight into her heart.

Christina felt herself blush. She'd never been so instantly attracted to anyone since . . . well, she'd *never* been so instantly attracted to anyone. It was *terrifying*.

"How about tomorrow night?" Andy asked. "Wouldn't it be nice to have a delicious meal after a hard day's work in a toy shop?"

Christina checked to see if he was being sarcastic about the "hard day's work" bit, but his smile was genuine.

"All right," she conceded. "Yes, it would be lovely to go out to dinner."

"Great! Should I pick you up here?"

"Um, no. I'll need to go home to drop off some things." *And,* she thought, *take a shower, change clothes, put on lipstick, eyeliner, perfume . . .*

"What's your address?"

"Five Milk Street. It's in town, just off Main Street, actually, although the streets are awfully curvy and not always well marked so it can be easy to miss. Do you know where the Maria Mitchell museum is? It's on Vestal Street, just after my house—" *You're babbling!* her IC—her Inner Christina—shrieked. *Shut up!*

Andy smiled. "I know where Milk Street is. I've been walking around the town a lot recently."

"Oh. How nice." *Could you sound any more insipid?*

"How about seven o'clock? Is that a good time for you?"

"Yes. Perfect. I'll see you at seven tomorrow night." *Now go away,* her IC thought, *because I'm about to giggle like a schoolgirl. But don't go away, because I want to stand here and just look at you.* Obviously, her Inner Christina was as dazzled as she was.

"See you then." With a wave, Andy opened the door and left the shop.

3

"You have a date with Andy Bittlesman?" Harriet was about to pop a vein. "How did you manage that?"

The Shedders were gathered in Mimi's eating lunch.

"Don't sound so surprised," Mimi told Harriet. "Christina's not exactly a dog."

"No, she is not," Jacob seconded quietly.

"How did you meet him?" Harriet demanded. "Why did he come in your store? Why didn't he come in mine? Mine is much more his class."

"His *class*?" Mimi rolled her eyes. "Oh, please, Harriet. You're a merchant. He's a zillionaire."

Christina took a bite of her turkey and cranberry sandwich and listened happily as her friends squabbled. Life was normal. Outside, the day was sunny. She'd done a good amount of business already today.

"He came in with his sister," Christina explained. "Who, I might add, is a patronizing snob. She threw the presents we gave Wink at me and pretty much said her daughter's too good to accept gifts from a peasant like me. This isn't a real date. Andy's trying to make up for his sister's behavior."

"Is he as handsome as he looks in the pictures?" Harriet demanded.

"What pictures?" Christina asked.

"You know, *N Magazine* and *Mahon About Town*. At art openings and the opera and so on."

Christina took a sip of her bottled water. "I've never seen pictures of him. He's handsome, I guess, and really nice. I don't know why his sister is such a snot. Poor little Wink."

"Poor little Wink?" Harriet almost elevated off her chair. "Her grandfather is Oscar Bittlesman! He's hardly *poor*. Anyway, how can you even think of a kid when you have a date with Andy Bittlesman?" Harriet narrowed her glittering cat eyes. "Where is he picking you up? If he comes to your shop, maybe I can wait with you. I could meet him, too."

"To try to steal him away from Christina?" Mimi laughed heartily. "*Nice*, Harriet."

"Oh, for heaven's sake," Christina protested, wadding up her sandwich wrapper. "First of all, this is not a real date. Second, Harriet, you're welcome to him. He's not my type. Third, I'd better get back to my shop."

"Actually," Harriet murmured thoughtfully, eyes half-closed in plotting thought, "I gave Wink part of those presents. Andy might want to thank me, too."

Christina's grandparents had owned the large summer house on Milk Street in the middle of town. Her parents had inherited it, and now it was Christina's. She was an only child, and last year, her father had died from Parkinson's, and this year, in early February, Christina's mother had died of a heart attack. Christina knew the painful truth—her mother had been glad to leave this earth. Christina's parents had been deeply in love and her mother had been lost without her husband.

Christina inherited the house, and she understood how fortunate she was, to own a house, mortgage-free, on Nantucket. But she would have gladly lived in an attic if it could bring her parents back. She had been very close to both parents—the family had really been the Three Musketeers. Without them, she was lonely, and this Christmas she was sad. She and her parents had had a ritual of picking out an evergreen tree, wrestling it into its stand, untangling the lights, and hanging the ornaments. They'd played Christmas music on their old-fashioned CD player and enjoyed hot chocolate as they worked.

This year, Christina didn't have a Christmas tree. Somehow she just couldn't do it, not alone, not this year.

She did hang a wreath on the front door, a simple evergreen circle with one large red velvet bow.

"What a great old place!" Andy said when he came to pick Christina up.

"I know," Christina agreed. "Comfortable, practical, and homey. Not designer-certified at all." She pulled on her coat. "I get a bit bored with all the perfect blue and white décor I see everywhere now."

Andy grinned wryly. "Then I'll have to think of something to entertain you when you come to our house."

She paused, confused.

"I mean," Andy explained, "Delia had the house redecorated two years ago. All blue and white."

"Oops," Christina said, adding, "I'm sure it's charming."

They hurried through the cold wind out to his Range Rover. He held the door for her to step into the luxurious, leathery warmth.

"Well," Andy continued as he steered along the narrow streets, "after Mother died, Delia needed a project to cheer her up. Delia is a whirlwind of OCD. But I'm glad I have a sister and a niece. Tell me, do you have any siblings?"

"No. I wish I did. Both my parents died within the past year, and I miss having family around at Christmas."

"I'm sorry to hear that."

Christina nodded. "Thank you." She didn't want to let sadness set the mood this evening. More lightly, she said, "But I have several wonderful friends. And the entire town is almost like family."

At this time of year, when all the summer people were gone, traffic was easy. It didn't take long for them to arrive at their destination, a small but first-class restaurant, Fifty-Six Union. The hostess knew Christina and winked at her as she ushered them to an intimate table at the back.

"Are you a Nantucket native, Christina?" Andy asked.

"I was born here," Christina told him. "So that makes me a native. But I was born prematurely, when my mother and father were visiting my mother's parents. My grandparents lived here year-round. He was the principal of the school. She worked in a shop. I've always loved it here, but

I grew up in McLean, Virginia. My father worked for the government. My mother and I came to stay with my grandparents every summer. My father flew up when he could." She paused to smile a thank-you at the waiter who brought them glasses of wine.

Andy raised his eyebrow. "Was your father CIA?"

Christina laughed. "No, actually, he was an architect. He worked with a section of the government that specializes in renovating large institutional buildings."

"And your mother?"

"My mother taught kindergarten. She loved Christmas. My father had Parkinson's and went quickly. My mother followed a few months later. I don't think she wanted to live without him."

Andy was silent. "I'm sorry. You must miss them."

"I do."

"And you don't have any siblings, you said?"

"I don't. Mother never told me why. But I want a bunch of children!"

Christina felt herself blush. *Too much wine,* she thought, but she knew it was Andy's warm gaze.

"It must be nice for kids to live here. The beach in the summer, and they can bike everywhere. Christina, I think you are the only adult I know who bikes to work."

Christina laughed. "Lots of people here bike. My shop is such a short distance from my house."

"You love Nantucket."

Christina nodded. "That's true. That doesn't mean I haven't traveled. I went to Wheaton College in Massachusetts. After college, I spent a summer touring Europe with a couple of girlfriends. Now that I have the shop, I try to go into New York at least once a year to see a play and stroll through the museums. But in our high season, the busiest season, from May through October, and during the holiday season, I'm at my shop. I've run it for five years now."

"Because you like children?"

"Probably. It might be a genetic thing. I caught liking little kids from my mother. It's a pleasure, seeing children's faces, and adults, too, when they first enter my shop. It's an *experience* for them, it's like entering a new world. So different from simply looking through a catalog or online and cold ordering."

As she spoke, Christina watched Andy and silently approved. He was an easy companion, flattering her with his regard, paying attention to what she said, asking pertinent questions, gazing at her with what seemed like genuine admiration.

"And now you," Christina prompted. Her wine had eased her nerves. She hadn't slept well the night before. Her own personal video of Andy in her store, his smile, the lovely deep sound of his voice, all played over and over again, as if her mind just didn't want to let it go. Her Inner Christina told her she absolutely could not count on this evening amounting to anything at all, but here with him now, so close that they could reach out and touch, all common sense floated away. "Tell me about you."

They ate mussels in garlic and buttery broth as Andy told her briefly about his past. He'd grown up in New York, gone to boarding school and college in Massachusetts, and worked for his father's brokerage firm. He was thirty; he'd never married, although he'd been engaged. He went to Colorado and Switzerland in the winter to ski, but his brownstone townhouse in Brooklyn was his home.

"Although, to tell the truth, Brooklyn doesn't feel like home anymore." Andy took a sip of wine and leaned back in his chair.

Christina waited. She sensed he was debating with himself over how much he wanted to tell her. She sat back in her chair, too, quiet and ready to listen.

Andy hesitated. "Dad had a minor stroke three years ago. He came to Nantucket that spring to rest and recuperate. He'd owned the cliff house for years, for summer vacations, but for some reason, he now says he intends to live here year-round for the rest of his life. He's tired, he says. When our mother died six years ago, his zest for life seemed to leave him, too. Not that he wasn't always a cantankerous, critical, coldhearted workaholic. But Mother softened him. She made him have fun, whatever that could possibly be in his cranky life. And with computers, he can work from home."

"Where do you fit into the company?"

"I'm my father's right-hand man. I'll inherit the company. Delia will get an equal share in stocks." Looking down, he said, "I've always lock-stepped right along the path my father pointed me toward." Andy paused. "I've tried to be the man he wants me to be, and I've succeeded. But at a cost . . ." Lifting his eyes to Christina's, he suddenly smiled. "Have you ever done something you were certain you'd hate doing, only to find that you enjoyed it?"

"Sure I have." Christina answered briefly, not wanting

to break the flow of his conversation. *Well done*, her Inner Christina praised her.

"My sister and I took turns this year coming to the island, being with Dad, working with him, watching to see that he was okay. Delia liked being here in the summer, for the galas and the beach, but I realized I like being here all the time. Even on rainy days."

They paused as the waiter set their seafood casseroles before them and poured more wine.

"I've gotten involved with some conservation organizations. I've been walking around the island, getting to know it, and some of the people here. It's made me think about my own life. Being here on the island in the fall and winter . . . it's such a change of pace from the city. It's liberating."

Christina bristled slightly. "Many of the island's benefactors think they want to live here year-round. They join local boards and donate money . . . and they leave after New Year's Eve. You haven't been through a real winter yet," Christina warned him. "The first three months of the year can be bleak. Gale-force winds that make it impossible to get on or off the island, no matter how urgent the need. No real nightlife except for movies at the Dreamland and Theatre Workshop productions and maybe lectures at the library. But nothing like what New York City has to offer."

"Do you like it here in the winter?" Andy asked.

She took a moment to gather her thoughts. "It's quiet here in the winter, and I like that. I can catch my breath, read, watch television, go out with friends. There's a rhythm to life here. Summer is an enormous challenge. It's crazy busy. Work and parties and no time to sleep! I like it, though. It's very cool to see my summer friends return. Over the years I get to know families because they visit the store, and it's a delight to see how much taller the children are after a winter away, if a kid's two front teeth fell out, if a woman is pregnant." Christina put her elbows on the table, folded her hands, and leaned her chin on them, letting herself sink into her memories. "Sometimes the college girls who helped me in the summer have graduated, or fallen in love and come into the shop to show off their engagement rings and fiancés. The shoulder seasons with the Daffodil Festival in April and the Cranberry Festival in October bring in a different crowd. You should come for Daffodil weekend. It's so much fun, a parade of decorated antique cars out to 'Sconset, and then everyone has the most remarkable tailgate picnics and the dogs are wearing collars made of daffodils, and the cars are absolutely smothered with daffodils." Christina stopped. "I'm talking too much."

"Not at all. This is fascinating."

Christina took a deep breath. "Okay, then, I've scrambled the seasons, but I'll get back to winter. After Christmas, we have time to slow down, have dinner with friends, walk on the beach—even in a parka because the waves can be so magnificent. So I guess I have to say I love it here in all the seasons. I can't imagine living anywhere else."

Andy nodded. "It all sounds great. I haven't been here long, I know, but I feel like I *get* the island." He set down his fork, folded his arms on the table, and leaned forward, his face intense, his eyes shining. "I'd like to start a philanthropic fund to help the conservation groups on the island. Not just for the land, but for the ocean, too. The island is a microcosm of what's happening all up and down the East Coast. I'd like to see Bittlesman and Company pivot from making money toward giving money to organizations that need it. I want our company to make a difference in the world."

"What does your father want?"

Andy leaned back. Frustration darkened his eyes. "He's an old-fashioned man. He was raised to work hard and be frugal. For years, the high point of his life was being known as someone in the Forbes 400. His stroke made him reflect, but it's not in his nature to be generous."

I know, Christina thought, but kept that thought to herself.

"He wants me to stay in New York. He wants me to do all the personal meetings and schmoozing, to be the face of the company." Andy's fists tightened on the table. "I'd like to live here. I've told him that if I lived on the island, I could be here for him, check in with him now and then, even though our housekeeper, Mrs. Harris, seems quite competent and is surprisingly kind and patient with him. I think I could tear him away from his computer and his obsession with making money and help him realize the pleasure of generosity."

"Are you saying you're thinking of living here permanently?" she asked.

"I am."

A shadow passed over his eyes. She said softly, "But something is holding you back."

Andy took a few bites of the casserole. She liked it that he took his time before answering.

"I don't want to make my father so angry he has a heart attack. But I don't want to live in the city. And I don't want to marry Anastasiya Belousova so I can attract more tycoons to invest with our company."

Christina gasped. "Whoa. How did we get to Anastasiya Belousova?" She'd seen the model's pictures on the front of all the fashion magazines.

"I was engaged to her."

Okay, Christina thought, *that's the kind of woman Andy Bittlesman dates.*

"She's a model."

"I know."

"So she's used to a certain type of life. Private planes to Aruba, Christmas in Paris, that sort of thing. In a way, Anastasiya's like my father. She has always worked hard, and she thrives on having the best of everything at her fingertips. Pouilly-Fuissé and oysters from room service at the Plaza. Private jet with friends to ski at Aspen. Seats at the Oscars."

"I've seen her face in magazines," Christina admitted. "She's very beautiful."

"True. She's also always hungry and dissatisfied with her looks. She's twenty-seven and in despair because she's so old."

Christina laughed but suddenly went serious. "I shouldn't laugh. I know that can be a real problem among women. Does she like Nantucket?"

Andy grinned ruefully. "Yes, she does. For about two

days in August, when she's got lots of galas and parties to attend."

"You make her sound shallow, Andy, but you must love her if you were engaged to her."

"I did love her. She's nice, and smart, and clever. She's not just a thoughtless mannequin. We got along really well when we were in her world. And I have to admit, it's glamorous to date a top model. When we were together, life was exciting. I felt glamorous by association. But I couldn't keep up with the whirlwind of her life, and she disdained the quiet of this island life. I guess the truth is that I changed, partly because I got tired of everything that she lived for. And she didn't want to give up all the glitz and prestige to walk on brick streets that snagged her high heels. We broke it off this summer."

"Do you miss her?"

"I don't think so. Being with her was like being in a hot air balloon or on a roller coaster. It's fun for a while, but you wouldn't want to live your life there. At least I wouldn't. To be honest, she was exhausting." Andy grinned. "Enough about all that. What about you? Why aren't you married yet?"

Christina shrugged. "I haven't met the right man, I guess. I did date a guy on the island for a long time. Jamie Locke. We really liked each other. We saw each other every summer, and it seemed we knew everything about each other. Maybe that's why, no matter how hard we tried, we couldn't be more than friends."

"Where is he now?" Andy asked.

Christina smiled and looked at her watch. "I imagine

Jamie's at home with his wife, Patty, trying to get their two-year-old twins to go to bed."

They laughed together. *I hope Anastasiya moves to the moon*, Christina's IC thought.

After dinner, they walked down Union Street to Main Street, admiring the window displays.

They stopped to study the books in Mitchell's Book Corner. The soft glow of the lamps and the small lights on the Christmas trees lining the streets illuminated the brick sidewalk.

Andy said, "I have a letter for you."

"A letter? For me? How odd."

Andy took it out of the breast pocket of his wool overcoat and handed it to Christina.

The letter was on Oscar Bittlesman's letterhead, which stopped Christina's heart for a moment. Oscar Bittlesman, or his enormous company, owned her shed.

Surely Oscar Bittlesman wouldn't have his son deliver a business letter about a rent hike in such a casual manner.

She unfolded the letter. The words were written in blue magic marker, in a tidy, uneven print.

Dear Christina,

I would like to work with you in your shop every day. Not for the entire day, just for a few hours when you are really busy. I know how messy the shelves get after a crowd of people has come through. I am a tidy person. I possess my own feather duster. I could bring that to your shop. (Not that I think your shop is dusty.)

I would be grateful to be paid five dollars a day for three hours of work. Or whatever you think is appropriate.

Your Friend,
Wink Bittlesman Lombard

Christina smiled. "Did you see this?"

She handed it to Andy, who quickly read it.

"She's a Bittlesman, all right," Andy said. "Nine years old and negotiating for pay."

"What would Delia say if I agreed to this?"

Andy shook his head. "Honestly, I'm sure she'd be grateful. Okay, scratch that, my sister is rarely grateful. But she's got to keep going into the city for this divorce mess. Our father, the old curmudgeon, hides himself away in his office all day. I'm spending as much time on the island as possible so I can be here for both of them." He handed the letter back to Christina. "I've taken Wink to Great Point and I've played Monopoly with her, but I'm afraid I bore her."

She tapped it against her lip, thinking. "Actually, she could be of some help. What worries me is my responsibility. I mean, what if she wanders off and doesn't return and I don't know where she's gone?"

"She's a serious little girl," Andy said. "We could stipulate that she can't leave the shop during her work hours."

Christina threw back her head as she exploded with laughter. "*Stipulate*! To a nine-year-old girl!" Smiling, she linked her arm with Andy's and started back to his car. "Tell her that if it's okay with her mom, she is welcome to work with me." She glanced up under her lashes at Andy. "Why don't you help her draw up a contract? *Stipulating* hours, salary, and the number and duration of bathroom breaks."

Andy grinned. "I think it will do her a lot of good to hang out with you."

Christina nodded. "I *concur*."

Walking back along Orange Street and down Mulberry Street to Andy's car, they held hands. Through the leather of his gloves and the wool of her mittens, Christina felt the surge of their physical attraction. She thought he would kiss her. She wanted him to kiss her.

But he drove her home, walked her to the door, and politely refused to come in for coffee.

"I know you have to work tomorrow," he said. "But I'd like to see you again soon."

"I'd like that, too," Christina said. *Go in the house*, her IC ordered her. *Don't stay here gazing at him like a lovesick teenager!*

"Thank you for a lovely night," Christina said, and gave Andy a little wave and went, alone, into her house.

4

December was always a crazy month. Christina's Toy Shop kept her running, waiting on customers, unpacking inventory, organizing the shelves, keeping track of sales on credit cards and sales in check or cash, rushing to the bank. The town held lots of festive events, and it seemed everyone Christina knew had a Christmas party.

Wink showed up at the shop at precisely one o'clock.

When Wink arrived, Christina was already surrounded by customers. At the back of the store, a couple was arguing about the moral impact of pirates. The husband wanted to buy his son several pirate items. The wife said pirates were nothing but thieves and she didn't want their son to think stealing was okay.

Two other customers were in line, waiting for Christina to ring up their purchases. Wink slipped down the narrow aisle between shoppers with the grace of an otter. She slid the contract onto a shelf in Christina's inner space behind the counter. She swooped to the counter on Christina's right, an array of small bins filled with petite, attention-catching items: white rope bracelets, marbles, miniature fairies, seashell angels, glass whales, and tiny, exquisite mermaid dolls.

During the past rush hour, all the minuscule objects had gotten mixed up in the bins. Wink set about organizing them.

Of course, the sight of a child so seriously moving the objects drew the customers' attention.

"Stocking stuffers!" one woman cried, and even more people clustered around Wink.

While Wink was there, Christina sold a pile of marbles, dolls, and whales.

After an hour, the store emptied out. *Do I dare?* Christina wondered. She always locked her shop when she had to rush across the wharf to the bathroom at the end of the shingled shops. She had to trust Wink . . . and she had to use the bathroom!

"Wink, I'm going to run to the restroom. It's right over there—"

"I know where it is."

"Good. Could you come behind the counter and stand right here by the cash register? If someone comes in, tell them I'll be right back."

Wink's shoulders straightened. "Don't worry. I know what to do."

Christina raced off to the restroom at the side of the dock.

When she returned, Wink was still behind the counter.

Two teenagers were debating over which wooden ferry to buy for their brother.

"Does your family come to the island with a car?" Wink asked.

"Yes," the teenage girl replied. "At the beginning of the summer. We take it back when we leave in the fall."

"Then you don't want the ferry you're holding. That's the fast ferry. You need the bigger car ferry. The one in the corner."

"Oh, right! That's smart. Thanks." The girl picked up the wooden replica of the *M/V Eagle*. "We'll take this one."

Wink sleekly slid out from behind the counter and Christina slid in to ring up the sale. When the customers left, Christina said to Wink, "It's a good thing I'm not paying you on commission!" She was sure Wink knew what *commission* meant.

Whenever the shop was empty, Christina and Wink scurried about tidying and restocking the shelves.

"Have you met any kids your age?" Christina asked one bright afternoon.

Wink didn't speak. She merely shook her head.

"The town puts on a Christmas pageant at the Congregational Church. I'm sure they could use another angel."

"I'm not an angel. And we don't go to church."

"Too bad. Churches are gorgeous this time of year. Have you seen the Festival of Trees?"

"I've seen the trees on Main Street."

"Inside the Whaling Museum, there are dozens of trees decorated in all sorts of fabulous ways."

"That's nice," Wink said softly.

"Maybe your mother could take you. I'm sure she'd enjoy it."

"I don't know when she's coming back to the island."

"Well, what about asking your grandfather to take you?"

"He doesn't exactly get into the holiday spirit." More quietly, she added, "Plus he's not wild about doing things with me."

"Maybe your uncle . . ." Christina began.

"Maybe you could take me," Wink suggested in a voice so quiet it was almost a whisper.

"Hmm," Christina said. "I think that's a great idea! Let me check the calendar and we'll make a date."

Wink began humming Christmas carols as she worked.

Even with Wink's help, Christina worked hard that day. When she arrived to the silence of her home, she collapsed on the sofa. Mittens, her enormous mixed-breed cat, immediately jumped on her belly and purred loudly, glad Christina was home. Christina put her feet up on a pillow and closed her eyes, relaxing.

Of course that was the moment her cell buzzed.

She glanced at the caller ID. It was Andy, so she should take the call, because it might be about Wink.

Who was she kidding? She would take the call because it might be Andy asking to see her again.

Andy had a lovely voice. "I know you were busy today. Wink told me. How about dinner tomorrow night?"

"I have a better idea. How about you take Wink

shopping for some pretty clothes, and then we'll all three go to the Festival of Trees at the Whaling Museum, and then we'll go out to dinner?"

After a moment of silence, Andy said, "Um, I don't know how to take a little girl shopping for clothes."

"That's easy. Take her to Kidding Around on Broad Street and ask Erin to help you. Then take her to Murray's Toggery, second floor. Wink needs some shoes with sparkles."

"Okay, but all this is with the understanding that I get another date with you alone, without Wink."

"I'll sign a contract to that effect," Christina said.

Clothes may not make the man, Christina thought the next evening, but clothes make the girl happy.

Christina, Andy, and Wink were strolling through the enormous redbrick Whaling Museum, gazing in wonder at the magnificently or humorously decorated evergreens. Well, Christina thought, Wink was spending as much time admiring her reflection in the glass cases as she was admiring the trees. Wink wore a black velvet dress with white tights and sparkling red Mary Janes. She wore a glittering silver headband Christina had given her. She was almost beside herself with happiness.

"Uncle Andy," Wink said, "could we go eat? My eyes are full and my stomach's empty."

Christina and Andy laughed.

"Of course we can go now," Andy said. "I'm hungry, too."

They had spent at least an hour looking at the trees, and Christina had been on her feet all day, so she was delighted to head over to the Brotherhood for dinner. They were settled at a table near the fire. Christina and Andy ordered bistro steak frites and local beers. Wink ordered the fried fish dinner so she could get the curly fries.

Andy allowed Wink to have ice cream for dessert—it was a special kind of day.

"How is your Christmas tree decorated?" Christina asked Wink.

Wink shrugged. "We don't have a Christmas tree."

"You don't have a Christmas tree?" Christina nearly fell off her chair.

"Granddad said he never gets one."

"Okay, but *you're* here now, Wink. And your mother will be back from the city pretty soon. And, Andy, where are you spending Christmas?"

Andy smiled. "I'm not sure. I was planning to go skiing in Colorado, but I think I might want to spend Christmas here, with my sister and my niece and . . . my father."

"Oh, please please please!" Wink begged, her upper lip coated with a mustache of whipped cream.

"What do you think, Christina?"

"It's not my place to say. Christmas is a family occasion," Christina began, but she could feel Wink's hopeful eyes fastened on her. "So I think of course you should spend Christmas here."

"Yay!" Wink cried. "So what's your Christmas tree like?"

"Um," Christina hedged a moment. Finally she admitted, "I don't have mine up yet. I've been so busy with work."

"Oh, goody!" Wink said. "We can help you decorate your tree and you can help us decorate ours."

"Okay," Christina agreed. "But first, do you have any ornaments?"

Wink's face fell. "At home, Mom always had the florist decorate our tree. I'm sure Granddad doesn't have any."

"Wonderful!" Christina said. "What fun you're going to have. You can buy some, and you can make some." With a slightly mischievous smile, she said, "I'm sure your uncle Andy will enjoy stringing popcorn and cranberries."

Later that evening, after Christina said goodbye to Wink and Andy, she took the flashlight out of the kitchen drawer and carried it with her up to the attic. There was a light up there, one poor lonely sixty-watt bulb with a string hanging down to turn it on and off. The attic was enormous, and packed with papers, clothes, and memorabilia of the Antonioni family.

Christina was sure there were boxes of Christmas ornaments up here, too. Her family had always come here for Christmas, and her parents had always gone wild with decorations. She hadn't intended to put up a tree this year, her first Christmas ever alone in the house. But the thought of Wink seeing Christina's house without a tree seemed just wrong. Maybe she would get a small tree. She sat on the attic floor and opened the first box.

Wow. Memories swirled around her like mist. Here were the ornaments she'd made with her mother every year when she was a child: red felt stuffed with cotton, cut to shape a snowman, Santa Claus, a bell, or a sled, sewn with green yarn around the edges, and embellished with glue and glitter. Christina held each one, remembering the love and the patience her mother had shown.

There were fancy store-bought ornaments, too, shiny crimson balls and porcelain snowmen, swans, and reindeer. Even the misshapen decorations Christina had made at school every year had been saved in the box.

She pulled out an oval ornament edged in stiff red lace. Turning it around, she saw that it was a picture frame, and the picture was of Christina when she was eight or nine and wore her hair in pigtails. She touched the picture and let memories sweep over her. Baking Christmas cookies with her mother. Sitting around the fire with her parents and grandparents, drinking eggnog and listening to Christmas music. Waking up on Christmas morning and allowing herself a delicious long moment of anticipation before running down the stairs to see what Santa had brought.

Of course she no longer believed in Santa, but she did believe in fate. And in true love. For a moment, she curled up, leaning her head against a cardboard box, and let herself remember the man she had thought she would marry. Jamie. He was such a good guy. She knew she could have had a pretty nice life with him. But she hadn't loved him in the dizzy-headed, heart-pounding, head-over-heels way she wanted to love someone, so she let him slip away.

"You'll never get married at this rate," Christina's mother had scolded her. "Stop being so picky."

"Mom, I want to fall into true, deep, long-lasting love like you did with Dad."

"Not everyone gets that," her mother told her.

"We want to be sure you've got someone to take care of you," her father said.

Those were fighting words for Christina. "I can take care of myself!" she declared.

"Oh, honey, we know that," her mother told her. "It's the little things we worry about. Like who will bring you aspirin when you have the flu. Or who will meet you at the ferry after you've gone off for a day's shopping."

Christina's mother had a gift for knowing that the small, seemingly inconsequential things mattered. Maybe that was why she'd taught kindergarten. Or maybe she'd taught kindergarten because she liked dealing with what seemed to adults like the easy little matters. Tying shoe-laces. Being gentle with small creatures like gerbils and hamsters. Singing at the top of your lungs, dancing in a circle, shaking all about. Laughing. Naptime, when the world settled down and you lay on your mat like a seal in the warm sand. Learning to share—not an easy lesson. The mystery of flour and water and baking soda. Honoring the seasons and all the holidays, Ramadan and Hanukkah and Passover as well as Christmas and Easter. The age-old alphabet song.

Her mother had always cared about the normal matters of the home as well. Now that she was older, Christina understood that it was a talent her mother had been born with, to focus on the present, to polish the everyday details of life, like she polished the toaster and teakettle before she left for work so that when she returned home, she found them gleaming at her like brand-new gifts.

Christina's father had been so different. He was an active, tense man, always worried, his forehead set in wrinkles like a dry desert floor. He worried about his work, about the state of the world—not one day passed when he didn't worry about the state of the world. When Christina made good grades, her father worried that she wasn't socializing enough; when she spent time with friends, her father worried that her homework wasn't getting enough attention.

Most nights, when Christina's father came home in time for dinner, he was fretful and absentminded, but Christina's mother could calm him down. Some nights, when he came home from work late, he would be so wound up he couldn't eat. Christina would eat alone in the kitchen while her mother sat in the living room, letting her husband vent about the craziness of the world.

Christmas was wonderful because the family came to the island to stay with Christina's grandparents. They were always so happy to see their granddaughter, and they were mad about Christmas—church, Santa, turkey, presents, and snow. The whole thing. It didn't matter so much if Christina's father spent half the time shut in another room talking on the phone to Washington.

When the family came to the island every summer to stay with Christina's mother's parents, Christina's father calmed down and actually enjoyed himself, for almost two weeks. Sometimes he walked on the beach with her.

Sometimes he took her into town for ice cream. Sometimes as they sat in the backyard eating dinner at the long table with her grandparents, *sometimes* Christina's father would laugh. Sooner or later, he would get a phone call, or later, a fax, or later, an email, and he'd frantically pack his bag and leave for Washington.

Christina didn't know how her mother could live with such a nervous man. But she did know, in the way children know without words, that her mother loved her husband and that he loved her. Often, when she was going through a tough time, she thought her mother loved her husband more than she loved Christina.

I won't marry a man like my father, she'd decided. *I won't marry an important man. You miss too much of life rushing around being important.*

With tears in her eyes, Christina forced herself back to the present. Opening the lid to a white box, she discovered a dozen paper snowflakes, each one crisp and unique. What fun she'd had the year she learned to fold a piece of white paper in half, cut in and out and carefully snip out diminutive triangles and circles, and unfold it to find an elaborate snowflake.

The cookie cutters were still in the utensil drawer. The recipes for the Christmas cookies and the gingerbread people were there, too, in a three-ring notebook. So were the scissors.

She could buy white paper from Nantucket Office Products.

Island Variety had lots of crafts material—sparkles and beads and felt . . .

She wondered if they still sold the artificial snow in a can that could be sprayed on a window to make a bell or a snowman or an angel.

Suddenly, she had an idea.

5

The next morning, she called Andy with her plan. That evening after her shop closed, she and Wink hurried to Andy's waiting car.

Christina took the passenger seat so she could show Andy where to turn. Wink sat in the back, leaning over Christina's shoulder.

"Seatbelt, Wink," Andy said.

"Aww. But I can't see as well back here."

"This car doesn't move until you've buckled your seatbelt."

Grumbling beneath her breath, Wink fastened her seatbelt.

"Go out Orange Street till you come to the rotary, then go left," Christina said.

"I bought a tree stand at Marine Home Center," Andy told her.

"Great! I found ours up in the attic. And Wink"—Christina turned toward the backseat—"I found the recipe for Christmas cookies."

"I don't know how to cook," Wink said quietly.

"Well, you'll be *baking*, and it's really easy, and I'll show you how."

"Left here?" Andy asked.

"Right. I mean, yes, take this left."

Soon they were at Moors End Farm, wandering through a forest of evergreens of all sizes and shapes.

"Let's get a really big one for Granddad's house," Wink said.

While Wink and Andy concentrated on the tall trees, Christina studied the shorter ones, especially the pines with their wonderful scent. She wanted a tree she could handle by herself, without anyone's help, and that limited the size. But now that she was here, she knew she *needed* a Christmas tree in her home. An evergreen tree was a living, spiritual presence. So many nights of her life she had sat in the dark just looking at their Christmas tree with its small, glowing lights, while a deep peace floated over her. Now as she moved among the evergreens, a forgotten sense of anticipation and happiness and hope awoke in her heart. Tears came to her eyes.

She saw one medium-sized tree, an A-shaped, thickly branched tree. "Oh, you're perfect," she said.

"Christina!" Wink, all smiles and excitement, raced over and tugged her hand. "Christina! Look what we chose! Isn't it tall?"

"Goodness! And isn't it fat! You'll need to make lots of ornaments for that tree."

The Christmas tree guy helped Andy tie the big tree to the top of his car. Christina marked the tree she wanted.

"I'd like to pay for this now and come back later with my car," she told the clerk.

"We'll help you," Andy said.

Christina jumped. She hadn't realized he was so near.

"Oh, that won't be necessary . . ."

"No, but it will be easier, and fun. We'll pick it up tomorrow night. I'll help you get it in the stand. And for a reward, I'll take some of those cookies Wink's been talking about."

"It's a deal," Christina said.

The night was dark and cold as they drove back to town, but the Christmas lights around roofs and porches twinkled like stars. Main Street was breathtaking with its rows of small evergreens wrapped in lights. Andy was driving them to his father's house—Wink had begged for Christina to help begin the decoration of their tree. Christina was reluctant. She didn't know if grumpy Oscar Bittlesman would show his face and make a fuss because a stranger was in his house.

But she would be there because of Wink, and surely even unpleasant Oscar Bittlesman had a soft spot in his heart for his adorable granddaughter.

She didn't need to worry. Janice Harris, the housekeeper, informed them that Mr. Bittlesman had already had his dinner and gone upstairs to his study. And of course Mrs. Lombard was in New York.

Janice held the door open while Andy and Christina brought in the enormous tree. Wink followed carrying boxes of new Christmas lights. Christina could feel Janice's curiosity boring into her back. Janice was an island woman, widowed a few years ago, her two daughters married and living on the island. Janice's silver-gray hair was short but shaped in a pretty puffy shag, like a chrysanthemum. Her indigo cat's-eye glasses accentuated her blue eyes, and she always had a modest brush of blush on her cheeks and lipstick on her mouth. She was a pretty woman, trim and active, around fifty-five. Tonight she wore khaki slacks, a blue cashmere sweater, and pearl eardrops. Christina didn't know her well, but they were friendly as passing acquaintances. Janice had lots of acquaintances and even more friends. By midnight tonight, half the town would know that Christina was dating Andy.

Unless Christina could squash the gossip.

"Janice," she said sweetly, "did Wink tell you she's helping me in my shop this month?"

"Oh, yes," Janice replied. "Wink has been talking about you constantly."

"Tomorrow after work, we're going to bake Christmas cookies!" Wink said.

"Lucky girl," Janice said. "Maybe you'll bring me one?"

"Sure!"

The living room was large, with a fireplace tiled with marble and several sofas and chairs and tables and lamps and still plenty of space for the tree.

"Let's put it in front of the window," Christina suggested, "so people can see the lights when they drive by."

"Good idea."

Andy put the stand together, anchoring its three red legs firmly on the carpet. He picked up the tree and slotted it in place. Christina and Wink lay on the carpet, turning the screws that held the trunk firmly. The branches brushed their faces. Janice left the room, returning with a watering can with a long spout. She lay down between Christina and Wink.

"This tree drinks a lot of water," Janice told Wink. "Wink, let me show you how to do it, and then you can be the official tree waterer. Okay?"

Janice slowly, carefully, positioned the watering can so that when she tipped it forward slightly, the spout poured water into the tree holder. "Now you do it, Wink. Don't do it fast and don't let the water come all the way to the top or it might overflow and get the carpet wet."

Frowning in concentration, her tongue caught between her teeth, Wink gently tipped the watering can. The three of them were so quiet they could hear the water streaming out into the holder.

"Is that enough?" Wink asked Janice.

"Let me show you how to check. Dip your finger in, touch the bottom, and you'll feel how much water is there. That's right. Now feel your finger. It's wet to the second knuckle. That's perfect."

Wink grinned. "Thank you, Mrs. Janice." She started to sit up and knocked her head into a low branch, sending needles into her hair. "Oops."

"You have to crawl backward," Janice told her. "Like this."

Christina crawled backward, too, hoping Andy wasn't looking at her bum. This was not the most attractive position. She was glad when she was out from under the tree and could stand up.

"Well done," Andy said.

"The next job is all yours," Christina told him with a grin. "Stringing the lights."

Because the lights were brand new and tucked tidily into slots in their boxes, they weren't as irritatingly tangled as usual. Andy found an aluminum ladder in the kitchen pantry. Using that, he climbed to the top of the tree, settling the lights among the short branches. He handed them down to Christina, who wound the string around the high middle branches, then handed them to Janice, who wound them around the fat lower middle branches, and finally Wink circled the tree, placing the lights on the abundant low branches.

"It's like the tree's wearing a green tutu!" Wink laughed.

"I'm glad that's done," Andy said.

"Now we have to let it fall out," Janice said.

"Fall out?" Wink repeated, her forehead wrinkled.

"You saw how its limbs were compressed, pushed together? The tree needs time to relax."

"She's right," Christina agreed. She put her arms up, hands touching, then slowly brought her arms down to show how the limbs would fall.

"Oooh," Wink said, repeating Christina's movement.

"We'll decorate the tree tomorrow night," Janice told the little girl. Turning to Christina, she asked, "Would you like a drink? Some hot cocoa?"

"Thanks, but I've got to get home," Christina said. "Tomorrow's another busy day."

"And after work, we're going to bake cookies!" Wink added.

"I'll drive Christina home," Andy said.

"I'll come, too!" Wink cried.

"No, young lady, it's late for you," Janice said. "Let's go brush your teeth and get in bed. I'll come tuck you in and read you a story."

Wink made her shoulders sag dramatically in a show of disappointment, but she spoiled the act by breaking into a jaw-cracking yawn.

Christina kissed Wink's forehead. "Good night, sweetie. See you tomorrow."

In the car on the way to Christina's house, Andy said, "You're so nice to Wink. I don't know how to thank you."

"You don't need to thank me! I like that little girl a lot. I'm having fun with her."

"I can tell. But when her mother returns to the island . . ." Andy didn't finish his thought.

"Are you afraid I'll be abandoned?" Christina asked lightly. "Don't worry. I've got plenty of friends, although none of them is nine years old." She chuckled, but something stung her heart at the thought of losing the little girl's company.

"So I'll pick you up tomorrow night a little after six?" Andy asked.

Christina's brain froze. "You will?"

"So we can go out and get your tree."

"Oh, right! Yes. Good. Thanks! See you then. Thanks for the ride!"

The next morning while she ate a bowl of hot oatmeal sweetened with honey, she texted her friend Louise.

Can you come over Friday evening to help me decorate Christmas cookies? Bring Dora!

Dora was only seven, but she was a self-assured child who wore her curly black hair au naturel, sticking out of her head like spikes.

Louise texted back: *What time?*

Encouraged, Christina invited another friend who had a son. Before she left for work, she made several batches of sugar cookie dough, put them in the refrigerator, and did a quick wash and rinse of the cookie cutters. Then, while she was still charged with Christmas cheer, she sent a mass email to her friends, inviting them to a tree decorating party on Saturday night.

At lunch with the other Shedders that afternoon, Mimi said, "Christina, thanks for your invitation. I'll be there!"

"Yes," Jacob said. "I'll come, too."

Christina swallowed a bite of her tuna fish sandwich before asking Harriet, "How about you? Can you come?"

"Who else is coming?" Harriet asked, busily tearing the crusts off her sandwich.

"What you mean is, is Andy Bittlesman coming, right?"

Harriet didn't even blush. "Right."

"I don't know. I haven't invited him yet. But he probably will come, with Wink."

Harriet asked, "Wink's his niece, not his daughter, right?"

Christina grinned. "You don't want to have any stepchildren?"

"Don't put words in my mouth," Harriet snipped. She added, "Okay, I'll come."

When Andy picked Christina up that evening, it was pouring rain.

She shivered as she slid into the car. "I'm so glad I already chose the tree. We won't have to wander around in this downpour."

"I put the backseat down. I think we can put the tree in through the back hatch. We won't have to worry about tying it on top of the car."

"Didn't Wink want to come?"

"She's doing FaceTime with her mother."

"Oh . . . how is Delia?"

Andy shook his head. "Stubborn. So is Jeff, her husband. I don't see this ending before Christmas."

"But Wink . . ."

"Wink will be fine. If necessary, my sister can send Jeannette to help with Wink."

"Jeannette?"

"Delia's housekeeper and babysitter. Wink probably sees her more often than she sees her own mother. Don't scowl. Delia is on a lot of charitable boards. Wink, as you can tell, is just fine."

"Wink certainly has a lot of people in her life . . ."

"Try thinking of Mrs. Harris and me and Jeannette as the daffy aunts and uncles."

Lighten up, her Inner Christina ordered. Wink was not her responsibility. "Yeah, that works."

"Good, because I think you're becoming one of the daffy aunts."

"Oh, I think I can be a fabulous daffy aunt!"

At the Christmas tree farm, they hurried through the rain to the shed to pick up Christina's tree from a clerk in a dripping raincoat. Andy hefted the pine and gently installed it in the hatch of his car.

"Well done!" Christina said as they rushed to get in the car and out of the rain.

"I do a lot of things well," Andy said, giving her a sideways grin.

Ignore him, her Inner Christina whispered. All her life she'd fallen for adorable summer guys who left for college or travel at the end of the summer. She didn't need a botched romance at Christmas!

Andy carried the tree into her house. Christina placed the stand in front of the window, and together they got the tree firmly positioned.

"Thanks!" Christina said heartily.

They were standing very near to one another, of necessity. They both stepped back, heads cocked to the side, studying the tree to be sure it was straight.

"Looks good," Andy said.

"It does." Now that the tree was taken care of, Christina said, because it seemed the natural thing to do, "Would you like a drink? Some wine?"

"I would," Andy replied, his voice soft.

For one long moment, Christina and Andy stood looking at each other, caught in a moment out of time, when marvelous and unexpected things happened. Christina wanted, very much, to kiss Andy, *really* kiss him, but the name *Anastasiya* floated through her mind like a banner on a television newscast.

"I'll get the glasses," Christina said. "Make yourself comfortable."

"May I help?" Andy asked, keeping his gaze on her steadily, as if unwilling to let her move away.

"No, of course not, I'm only—" Suddenly she was flustered. Babbling. And she knew her cheeks had gone red. She wanted to jump the man!

She'd be lucky if she could make it to the kitchen without walking into a wall.

"I mean, would you prefer red wine or white? Or maybe coffee? Or tea?"

His smile was sweet. "Christina, I'd like a glass of wine. Red if you have it."

She nodded and left the room. In the kitchen, she bent over the sink and splashed her face with cold water. This kind of undeniable magnetism had never happened to her before. It thrilled her. And terrified her.

She took down two wineglasses and filled them with pinot noir. By the time she returned to the living room, she was composed.

Andy was sitting on the sofa, a magazine in his hand. "Thanks," he said, taking his glass.

Christina curled up in a chair across from him.

"It smells like Christmas in here," she said. "Thanks so much for helping me with the tree."

"You're more than welcome." Andy leaned forward.

Christina held her breath.

He held up the magazine. "I found an article in here about the coastal preservation association. I've been thinking of joining their board. What do you know about the group?"

Christina relaxed, sipped her wine, and took a moment to think. "I don't know who's on that board. Nantucket has several environmental conservation organizations. To be honest, everyone loves the island and wants to protect it, but not everyone agrees on exactly how to do that."

Andy nodded. "I think I understand. I've been on some boards in the city that raise funds for various museums and symphonies. But mostly those have been boards I feel obligated to be on because of my mother's interests." He drank some wine. "I've been thinking about our talk at Fifty-Six Union. I *don't* want to rush in here like some rich city guy and throw my money around and get my face in the paper. Maybe it sounds odd, or arrogant, but I think I've changed during the few months I've spent on the island—and I know my connection to this place can't compare with yours, or with that of anyone who grew up here."

Christina nodded, listening.

"I sailed here this summer," Andy said. He let out a long breath. "Sailing can be such a powerful experience, even on the quietest day. I'd go up into the Polpis Harbor, or out past the Jetties, and it seemed that everything in my life just fell away, like a weight slipping off my back. I was simply there with the clear water and the unpredictable wind. The sail would luff, and it was like a live thing breathing. The main sheet would tug in my hand like an invisible spirit. I've never felt more myself, and never been so far away from the man I've been for years."

"Andy, that's wonderful," Christina said. "You sound like a poet."

"I probably sound like a jackass," Andy said, grinning. "Just another guy who has an earthy-crunchy moment of bliss."

"No, you're wrong," Christina told him, and now she leaned forward. "Andy, lots of people summer here, sail here, play tennis here, because it's chic. So many guys I know—good guys, nice guys—sail because it's fun, and they toss back beers and capsize and right the boat and howl with laughter. I don't believe I've ever heard anyone talk the way you just did."

"You probably think I'm a nerd."

"I don't think that. I think . . . I think you're remarkable." *And here we go*, her IC groaned.

Andy rolled his eyes and relaxed deep into the sofa. "I don't usually talk so much. But I can tell how *you* feel about the island, so I can be bold enough to talk this way. My schoolmates, my friends, even my former girlfriends, including Anastasiya, are crazily competitive. They drive themselves hard. If the Dow is down, they act like their dog died, they get plastered and curse and cry—it's not pretty. And my father . . . when I was growing up, he wasn't around much, but when he was home, Mom and Clara, our nanny, would sort of shove us upstairs to our rooms. They'd even bring our dinners up because they didn't want to risk us doing something wrong and making Dad even more angry.

And the guy Delia married, Wink's dad, is just like our dad. I hate that for her."

"Wink's lucky she has you for an uncle."

"Is she? I'm not so sure. It seems to me what Wink could use in her life is some security. Continuity. A stable home. Delia's marriage is in turmoil right now. My father sold his Park Avenue apartment when he came here, so the place where Wink spent time as a little girl is gone."

"Children don't remember much from their early years," Christina told him. "And Delia and her husband . . ."

"Jeff."

"Even if Delia and Jeff are having trouble now, they must have been pretty good parents to have a little girl as happy and confident as Wink."

"You're right."

"Wink is *their* daughter, after all. You said you want to be Goofy Uncle Andy." Christina grinned.

Andy laughed. "I did. I am." He finished his wine. "I should go and let you get some rest."

They both rose. "Andy," Christina said, "Friday night I'm having a couple of friends with children over here to help me decorate Christmas cookies. In my family, we always made some extra gingerbread men and women and sugar cookie stars and poked small holes in their heads to put ribbon through. Then we'd hang them on the tree. So Saturday night, I'm going to have a tree decorating party. I'd love it if you could come both nights. Or either."

"Sounds great. I'll come both nights, and I'll bring Wink."

"Good."

For another moment they stood smiling at each other, as if time had hit a pause button, and then Andy leaned forward and kissed Christina softly on her mouth.

"Forgive me for talking so much," he said.

"Nothing to forgive. I enjoyed it." *I enjoyed the kiss, too*, Christina wanted to say, but her Inner Christina wouldn't let her. "I'm glad you talked. I'm glad you're coming to the parties. I'm glad you and Wink got me into the Christmas spirit."

"Me, too," Andy said.

They stared at each other for another long moment before laughingly forcing themselves to look away. Christina walked Andy to the door, and stood watching him as he got into his car and drove off, the taillights of his car blinking like stars.

6

A lull often fell in the second week of December, as shoppers recovered from the excitement and extravaganza shopping of Stroll Weekend. Not many customers that Friday—bad. Lots of energy for her cookie party tonight—good!

On her way home from work, Christina stopped at the grocery store to buy every kind of decoration imaginable. Sprinkles, silver balls, confectioner's sugar, food coloring, and icing bags. At home, she changed into yoga pants and an old flannel shirt of her father's. She put on some light-hearted Christmas music about chipmunks wanting their two front teeth. She rolled out the refrigerated cookie dough and mixed up another batch.

She was finishing the first bowl of icing when Louise and Dora arrived. And then her childhood best island friend Allen and his son, Chad, who was eight and had a mild form of autism, came in. Chad would probably stand in the corner of the kitchen staring down at the floor, but at least he would be out of the house and among friends doing fun things.

Andy arrived with Wink.

Wink's eyes widened when she saw the other girl. She reached for her uncle's hand. Andy frowned, curious.

"Hi, guys!" Christina swept over to Wink, knelt in front of her, and kissed her cheek. "I decided it would be more fun if we had a little party. Can you stay, Andy? Wink, come and meet Dora." Christina knew not to gawk at the two girls, watching to see if they liked each other. "And this is Allen, and that's his son, Chad, over in the corner," which she knew from experience was the only way Chad was comfortable meeting new people.

"And I'm Louise, Dora's mom," Louise said to Andy, cocking her head and looking him up and down with a smile on her face.

"Nice to meet you." Andy shook her hand.

"Much nicer to meet you," Louise joked.

"Pay no attention to her," Christina said. "She's shameless. Right. I've made eggnog for the adults," she told them, "with a slight bit of rum, the way my parents made it. It's in the refrigerator. Help yourself. I've got to take a sheet of cookies out of the oven. For the kids, just water. I have a feeling they'll be enjoying enough sweet stuff."

For a moment, the group stalled, and then Christina put the first row of cookies on waxed paper, and Dora and Wink began a serious discussion of which colors to make the bell and the star and the snowman, and Allen asked Andy if he had just moved to the island, and Andy explained his situation, including the fact that his last name was Bittlesman, and conversation stalled again for a moment.

Louise broke the silence. "Where's the Christmas music?"

"I've got it right here," Allen said, tapping his phone.

The cheerful tune of "Frosty the Snowman" flowed through the air.

"Perfect," Christina said. "Okay, let's get busy. Everyone gather around the kitchen table. I've made several piles of cookies. We've got four colors of icing—red, white, green, and blue. You can use an icing bag, but I find a knife works as well. We've got lots of sprinkles. I have dibs on putting ribbon through the holes for hanging on the tree. Sometimes people get a little carried away with the holes." She grinned at Louise. Last year, Louise had had a cookie decorating party and two boys had decapitated Santa and a gingerbread man.

They set to work. The girls concentrated on their cookies, murmuring to each other. Allen took a cookie on a plate and a small bowl of icing and set it on the floor in front of Chad, who squatted down and carefully, slowly iced his cookie.

"So this must be the first time you've ever been in a kitchen," Louise said to Andy with a smug smile.

Christina opened her mouth to object. Louise was always a mischief maker, from kindergarten on, but this was insulting.

Before she could speak, Andy said, "Yes, that's true. I've never been in a kitchen. We always had Cook prepare our meals. We had seven dining rooms, because Mother found it just too boring to eat in the same room every day. Of course we had dogs for tasters, in case someone wanted to poison us. We lost only three or four dogs that way."

Both girls and even Chad were staring at Andy as if he'd grown another head.

Then Wink said, "Uncle Andy, that's not true! You're just being silly!" Looking around the table, she said, "We've never had dogs. Mrs. Janice cooks for us here, and Mommy cooks in the city and sometimes when Uncle Andy makes pancakes he lets me stir the batter."

"Oh, dear," Louise said. "Andy, I owe you an apology. I was trying to bait you."

"No apology necessary," Andy told her. "We did have a cook while my mother was ill, and my father hired Janice Harris to be his cook and housekeeper now that he's older."

"Janice Harris?" Louise asked. "*Our* Janice Harris?"

Andy looked puzzled.

Allen spoke up. "Louise means that Janice is an islander. Born here, grew up here, married and raised her children, and was widowed here. She's a wonderful woman. Knows everyone in town. Helps with voter registration. Takes library books to shut-ins. A treasure."

"I'm surprised she's working for Mr. Bittlesman," Louise said, and the joking tone had left her voice. "I didn't know she needed money. I mean, she's not wealthy, but I thought she was doing okay."

"Maybe she was bored," Christina suggested.

"But she has a zillion friends," Louise countered.

"That's not the same as having a job. Janice likes to keep busy."

"You'd better watch what you do," Louise warned Andy. "Janice keeps no secrets to herself, and you all would make great gossip."

Christina bugged her eyes out at Louise. What had gotten into her friend?

Before she could say anything, Wink held up an angel iced in blue with glitter on her wings. "Mrs. Harris asked me to bring her a cookie. I made this for her."

"That's beautiful, honey," Louise said. "Dora, want to make one for Daddy?"

The child's sweetness changed the mood of the room. Allen asked Andy if he sailed, and the two men bonded about boats and winds and shifting sandbars and windsurfing. Christina and Louise supervised the girls while Christina ran a red ribbon through the cookies so they could hang on the tree. Chad sat in the corner, icing his cookie with great concentration, his tongue between his lips. Christina exchanged a look with Allen; they both smiled. Chad was happy.

By nine o'clock, the children were fading, even though they'd had plenty of sugar. Allen and Chad left, Louise and Dora left, and Andy helped Wink get into her coat. They all had paper bags full of decorated cookies in their hands, and even Christina's teeth ached from eating too much sugar.

"I like your friends," Andy said.

"Good! You'll see them again at my Christmas tree decorating party tomorrow."

Wink piped up. "Is Dora coming?"

"You bet. In fact, Dora's mom wanted to know if you

could sleep over at Dora's house tomorrow night. It's Saturday, so no school the next day."

Wink's eyes widened. She tugged her uncle's hand. "Can I, Uncle Andy, can I?"

"*May* I," Andy reminded her. "Of course, although I'm not sure when your mother's coming home. She might want to spend the evening with you if she flies home on Saturday."

"Oh, I can see her anytime," Wink said heartlessly. "Please please please, Uncle Andy!"

"Okay," Andy said. "Christina, I'll get phone numbers tomorrow."

Christina kissed Wink's cheek. On a whim, she kissed Andy's cheek, too. If Wink hadn't been standing right there, Christina thought she would most certainly have kissed his mouth.

7

Saturday the weather turned unseasonably mild. Shoppers rushed out to shop while they knew they wouldn't get wet or slip on ice. The day passed in a blur of mermaids, pirates, Legos, ferries, rope bracelets, screaming children, hyperactive seven-year-olds, and a pretty little five-year-old who pulled the marble container over so that all the marbles rolled across the floor. Wink earned her salary that day. Quick as a, well, a *wink,* the girl dropped to her knees and gathered up the wayward marbles. After that, whenever a child came in, Wink sweetly showed the child a mermaid doll or a ferry, allowing the mother the freedom to concentrate on shopping.

At the end of the day, Christina said to Wink, "Choose anything you want from this shop. You deserve it!"

A small voice in the back of her mind warned her: *Don't let yourself get too close to this little girl. She's not yours.*

After Wink left, Christina shut and locked the door and turned the OPEN sign to CLOSED.

Then she slid right down onto the floor, rested her arms on her knees and her head on her arms.

She'd been trapped in this sort of bleak emotional cloud before over the past year so she knew she had to wait till it passed. She had to allow her Inner Christina to berate her for all her choices. All her friends were married, with children, or married with children on the way, and here she was, a thirty-year-old *spinster*. Okay, no one used that word anymore, but it sounded more demeaning than *single* and she was in the kind of mood a friend told her about: Sometimes you're so depressed you'll do anything to make yourself feel worse. She had always wanted to marry and have children and it broke her heart to know that she hadn't given her parents grandchildren before they died. But a person didn't get married just to have children, did she?

She lightly hit the back of her head against the door. *Christmas.* Such an emotional time. It was a joy for her to see children's faces light up when they spotted the perfect toy, and that joy filled her heart. But it was difficult then to return home to an empty house—okay, she had Mittens, but giving her a new catnip mouse for Christmas wasn't the same as being with a family.

Now she'd met Wink. And Andy. Was she falling in love with him? Of course not! He was a Bittlesman who dated models. He'd probably return to New York after Christmas and marry Anastasiya Belousova, and in a few years he and his wife would swan into Christina's small shed of a store with their many perfect children . . .

Okay! her Inner Christina announced. *Enough!*

She pushed up off the floor and set about readying the store for tomorrow. The work took her mind off her pathetic whining, and even cheered her, because she'd made a healthy bit of money during the day.

She hummed a Christmas tune as she gathered her things. Just then her phone pinged and she saw that she had a text from Wink. Christina took a moment to wonder how many other nine-year-old children had their own phones, and then she read the text.

Mom's back! She got here today! She's taking me out to get my hair cut and we're both going to get mani-pedis! XOXO

Christina felt like a child who'd been picked last for the volleyball team.

I told you! the smug little voice in her head said.

"Shut up," Christina said—no one else was in the shop.

Hi, Wink. That's great! Have fun! Bring her to the tree decorating party tonight. XOXO

Mom says we might have other plans.

I hate your mother, Christina thought sulkily.

But what she hated, really, she knew, was the sudden absence of Wink in her life. The party would be fun, but not quite as much fun if Wink wasn't there.

Christina walked along the wharf and her spirits lifted. Mimi was waiting for her at the Stop & Shop parking lot. Her SUV was stuffed with boxes of decorations and bags of food and wine.

"Mimi," Christina asked as she settled in the passenger seat, "how many Christmas sweaters do you possess?"

Mimi laughed heartily. "You don't want to know. At least ten, maybe twelve. You see, every year I get just a tad larger and last year's sweater doesn't fit, so I have to buy a new one."

"Why not give the old ones to the Seconds Shop?"

"Because I keep planning to lose weight," Mimi said. "But not tonight!" She laughed uproariously.

They drove to Christina's house and lugged in the boxes and bags. Last night Christina had strung the lights on the tree and brought down several boxes of ornaments from the attic. The gingerbread house she'd made years ago was, amazingly, intact, complete with peppermints, licorice sticks, M&M's, gumdrops, and snow made from confectioner's sugar and the secret ingredient that made the roof stay on the house: Elmer's Glue, which looked just like snow. The gingerbread house was really adorable. She put it in the middle of the dining room table.

While Mimi set the ornaments out on the coffee table, Christina covered the dining room table with Dutch and French cheeses, crackers, olives, chips and salsa, and a crockpot steaming with homemade chili. She put wine on the kitchen counter where small people couldn't reach and set paper cups next to an unbreakable jug filled with watered-down organic orange juice. Louise had warned Christina not to serve sugared juice to children; it would make them even more hyper.

Louise and Dora came first, followed by lanky Jacob, who had made miniature kites from Christmas wrapping paper to hang on the tree.

"Oh, Jacob! These are adorable!" Christina kissed his

cheek and pretended not to notice that he blushed bright red. "Come have some wine."

Other island friends, with or without children, streamed in the door, and soon they were gathered around the tree, decorating the fragrant pine with silver bells and scallop shells glued to red ribbons and angels, snowmen, snowflakes, and dozens of other ornaments.

Christina tried not to look at the door every five seconds, but she wondered where Wink and Andy were.

Then the door flew open and two people stepped inside, shaking raindrops off their parkas.

Wink. And her mother.

"Are we too late?" Wink asked.

"Never too late," Christina said. "Dora's here. Why not help her decorate the bottom of the tree? It's hard for us old people to get down there."

"Yay!" Wink skipped off.

"Welcome, Delia," Christina said, trying to inject some warmth into her greeting.

"Andy isn't coming. He had to fly back to the city." Delia dropped her parka on a chair and stood in front of the hall mirror, patting her hair into perfection.

Christina's heart sank. "Oh. Well." She didn't dare let on how disappointed she was. "But *you're* here! Come in and have a glass of wine or eggnog and meet everyone."

Delia looked like she'd rather have a root canal, but she followed Christina into the living room.

"Everyone!" Christina yelled. "This is Delia, Wink's mom. Introduce yourselves."

Bathroom, she mouthed at Mimi, who was refilling a plate of cookies.

In the privacy of the bathroom, Christina stared at her reflection. Her Inner Christina muttered, *Stop it. Get a grip. He's probably with the gorgeous Anastasiya. Grow up. Slap a smile on your face. Life goes on.*

Someone knocked on the door. Christina jumped.

"Christina," Mimi whispered. "Are you in there talking to yourself?"

Christina opened the door. "How did you know?"

"Hey, kid, when you get to be my age, you'll know everything." Mimi took Christina's hand. "Come on out and have fun with your friends."

Christina saluted Mimi. "Aye aye, cap'n."

She was surprised—no, shocked, really—to see that in the short time she'd been away from the living room, Delia and Jacob had struck up a conversation. *Delia and Jacob?*

Harriet sidled over to Christina. Keeping her eye on Jacob and Delia, she said softly, "Kind of makes you wonder, doesn't it?"

"I've always thought Jacob was hot, in a nerdy way," Christina said.

"Never mind his looks. If Delia Bittlesman Lombard is talking to Jacob, I'll bet Jacob has money."

"Why don't you investigate?" Christina suggested.

"You bet I will." Harriet wandered into the kitchen for another glass of wine.

The party was a smashing success for adults and kids. All the food vanished, every dish and paper cup and bowl was used, and the Christmas tree was a marvel, hung with so many ornaments it was hard to see the tree itself. No one got drunk and obnoxious, but everyone was exceedingly cheerful. People spontaneously began singing carols, Delia didn't leave Jacob's side, Wink and Dora got bored decorating and crawled into a corner to whisper secrets.

Christina's cat, Mittens, remained under the sofa, sending darts of rage at Christina whenever she passed by.

Gradually everyone left. Wink, beside herself with happiness, skipped off to spend the night with Dora as Louise shepherded the giggling girls out the door. Mimi carried plates into the kitchen, covered the few leftover cookies with plastic wrap, and put dishes in the dishwasher.

Delia and Jacob departed together. Harriet stood at the window, watching them talk as Jacob walked Delia to her car.

Christina approached Harriet. "Are you spying on Delia and Jacob?"

Harriet sniffed. "So what if I am?"

"I thought you weren't interested in Jacob because he's not rich."

"Good, because that's what I want you to think, but it's not what I think."

"Harriet, you're a very confusing person."

"You think I don't know that? You should try being me."

"So you like Jacob?"

"*Like?* I'm crazy about the guy. And look! There's hope, because as you can clearly see, Jacob responds to bossy women. Delia is certainly as difficult as I am."

"So you're trying to attract Jacob by being unpleasant?"

"I'm *not* unpleasant. I'm snobby, critical, and unkind, like rich women are. At least the women who come in my store."

"It certainly comes easy to you," Christina pointed out.

"Okay, I know I'm a pain in the neck. But I want to live on Nantucket, and I can't ever afford a house here, I can scarcely meet the rent on my hole of an apartment. I'm determined to marry someone wealthy. *You* don't have to worry about that, Christina. Your parents left you a house. *I* should be dating Andy Bittlesman, but he likes *you*."

"And now because Delia Bittlesman seems to like Jacob, you suspect he's wealthy."

Suddenly Harriet had tears in her eyes. "What does it matter, really, Christina? Jacob doesn't even know I'm alive."

"I'm sure that's not true."

"He won't even look at me."

Christina reached out to hug Harriet, but the other woman froze, so Christina only patted Harriet's arm. "So if Jacob doesn't like you, that means fate wants you to wait until the right man comes along. A rich man, right?"

"I wish my mind would tell my heart that." Harriet shook herself, and, as if coming out of a trance, she morphed into pleasantness. "Christina, this was a lovely party. Thank you for inviting me. I'll see you tomorrow at lunch."

"You're welcome," Christina said politely. She could tell that Harriet was regretting her moment of softness and her confession about Jacob.

She understood how Harriet felt. She had her own mixed feelings about Andy.

Mimi came out of the kitchen, rubbing lotion into her hands. "It's all done, sweetheart. What a great party."

"Oh, Mimi, you didn't have to clean up."

"I was happy to do it. You know me, I can't sit still." She pulled on her parka. "I know you're sad that Andy didn't make it. But he'll be back."

"I really liked him," Christina confessed.

"You really *like* him," Mimi said.

"He could have called. He could have texted."

"That's true." Christina didn't want to inflict her disappointment on her friend. "But hey, did you see how Delia latched onto Jacob?"

Mimi laughed. "I can't wait to see how Harriet acts with Jacob the next time we're all having lunch."

"Harriet likes Jacob," Christina said.

"Of course she does. That's why she acts like a fourth grader around him. And Jacob has no idea. Men. Some things never change."

Christina laughed with Mimi. She kissed Mimi's cheek, walked her to the door, and waved goodbye as Mimi drove away.

"Mittens? You can come out now." Christina used her most sweet, alluring voice. She needed someone—and her cat was more a some*one* than a some*thing*—to cuddle with while she thought about Andy. She curled up on the sofa and simply, for a while, looked at the Christmas tree, so extravagantly and eccentrically decorated by her friends, young and old. The warm scent of pine filled the room. The tree glowed, and Christina felt warmed by that glow. Accompanied by that glow, somehow.

She was fortunate. She knew that. It was ridiculous of her to feel so downhearted because of one man she scarcely knew. But she'd felt something special between them— a spark, a connection, and certainly desire.

That he couldn't even be bothered to call or text her that he couldn't come to the party was a big red warning sign. He had appeared to be considerate, but he didn't act that way. She remembered their discussion at Fifty-Six Union, how she'd gotten all defensive when he talked about helping the island. Maybe she'd put him off by her bristly reaction. But all her life, she'd seen people come to the island, fall in love with it, and then try to change everything about it. Maybe she'd overreacted. Maybe he thought that underneath her pleasant personality she hid a hot-tempered harridan.

"Stop!" she said, so loudly that the cat jumped out of her lap.

She would not sit here and blame herself for ruining a possibly important relationship. She would not allow herself to sit around like a teenager, making up excuses for Andy, trying to figure out why he'd been so very interested in her and then not even bothering to be polite enough to call.

She was an independent woman. And she had a shop to run tomorrow. She would go to bed now and not think about Andy anymore!

The next day was warm and sunny. Christina biked to her shop, thinking that this weather was, frankly, a bummer.

She liked cold, crisp air in December. It inspired the holiday spirit. She really wished it would snow.

Sunday mornings were often slow. Christina got a lot of
paperwork done and organized the shelves. She stood on a
ladder to hang the paper snowflakes she'd cut out, and
afterward, the shop looked much more Christmasy.

"Hi, Christina!" Wink walked in at one o'clock on the
dot.

"I didn't think you'd come today, not with your mother
on the island," Christina said.

"I told her I have a *responsibility*," Wink said seriously.
"Anyway, she's on the phone with lawyers all the time."

Wink handed Christina a bundle of white roses
wrapped in cellophane and tied with a red bow. "These are
for you."

Christina took them. "Thanks, but they've, um, wilted."

"I know. I told Mom they would. Uncle Andy told Mom
to take them to you at the party. Mom forgot."

Christina smiled wryly. "She forgot to put them in
water, too."

"And Uncle Andy had written a card, but Mom lost it.
I'm sorry."

"Wink, it's not your fault. Or your mother's. She has so
much on her mind." Knowing that Andy had bought her
flowers made it easy for Christina to be charitable. "I'll get
some water at the restroom and we'll see if we can revive
them." With a smile, she thought: *Just like the hope in my
heart has been revived by the wilted flowers.*

For the rest of the day, Christina and Wink were busy
unpacking boxes, checking off the inventory list, sticking

on price labels, and placing items on the shelves. Few customers came in, but when they did, they bought piles of
presents. It was a good day.

"Mom said she wants to ask you a favor," Wink said.

"She does?"

"You know the gingerbread house in the middle of your
table? Did you make it?"

"I did! Years ago. It's real gingerbread. But it's so old no
one could eat it now."

"Do you have, like, a recipe and instructions for making
it? Because Mom really liked your Christmas cookies, but
she wants to do something *extra special* with me."

Not that she's competitive or anything, Christina thought
with an inward smile.

"Of course," Christina said. "I've got the directions at
home. I'll snap a photo of them and send them to your
mom." With a crooked smile, she added, "I'll get your mom's
email address from your uncle Andy."

"Cool." Wink skipped away at four o'clock, while there
was still some light in the sky.

At six, Christina closed the shop. The poor wilted white
roses had not revived in the vase of water, but she wrapped
them in paper, laid them in the bike's basket, and took them
home anyway. She wanted to keep them until the petals fell
off. Roses from Andy! Although of course, they were really
for the Christmas party.

That night was a relaxing one for Christina, and she was
glad. She had presents to wrap and cards to send. She biked

to the Easy Street Cantina to pick up tacos to take home for dinner, which she ate in her robe while she zoned out on TV. She gave Mittens a special helping of treats, read part of a novel, and went to bed early.

She ordered herself not to think about Andy Bittlesman.

She thought about him anyway.

The next morning, she was in her shop, chatting with Freddy who brought the mail, when her heart sank.

At the top of the pile was a very business-looking envelope addressed to Christina Antonioni from Bittlesman and Company.

Inside, she found a letter informing her that her building and the other three buildings on the wharf had recently been purchased by Oscar Bittlesman. As of February 1, her rent would be raised by ten percent.

She couldn't breathe.

Her cell buzzed.

"Did you get the letter?" Mimi asked.

"Just now. I think my head exploded."

"Come here at lunch. We all must talk."

Christina texted Wink to tell her not to come in today. She might spend any free time on the phone with a lawyer or one of the Shedders and she didn't want the girl to hear her in a bad mood, and she was definitely in a bad mood.

*   *   *

Harriet, Jacob, Mimi, and Christina sat in a circle in the back of Mimi's shop.

"So we all got the same letter, right? Bittlesman's raising our rent by ten percent. That will take a huge chunk of our profits," Mimi said.

"He can't do this!" Harriet protested.

"Actually," Jacob said grimly, "he can."

"Is there anything we can do about it?" Christina wondered.

The three other merchants stared at her.

"What?" Christina asked.

"You're dating Bittlesman's son," Harriet pointed out.

"We're hardly *dating*," Christina said.

"Yeah, well," Harriet continued aggressively, "you had Delia Bittlesman and her kid at your party. It's on you to do something about this. Tell Bittlesman you'll stop babysitting his granddaughter if he ups the rent."

"Harriet! I'm not *babysitting* Wink! That little girl has nothing to do with—"

Mimi intervened. "This rent hike slams us all in the face."

"In the pocket, too," Jacob added.

"So we're all upset and emotional. Let's take a day or two to think of possibilities."

"I've got a *possibility*," Harriet snapped. "I'm going to buy a slingshot and learn how to use it, and when Bittlesman comes out of his house—"

"Stop that right now!" Mimi said. "It's Christmas."

"Yeah, well, Bittlesman sure does not have the Christmas spirit," Harriet grumbled.

The Shedders all returned to their stores. Even with her small space heater turned to high, Christina couldn't get warm.

Outside, night fell early. The Shedders usually kept their shops open until six in December, in case any island person who worked until five needed a chance to shop. But the wind was picking up. Waves were slapping against the pilings supporting the wharf.

Christina opened her door and looked out. Was it going to snow? It was certainly cold enough. But a crescent moon hung bright in a cloudless sky.

"Bah humbug," Christina said.

Just as she was cashing out, her cell rang.

"Christina!" Andy sounded full of good cheer. "I just got back to the island. Can I take you out to dinner tonight?"

Her heart rose—and she remembered her rent hike. "I'm sorry, Andy, not tonight."

"Does this have anything to do with my father?" Andy asked. When Christina didn't answer immediately, he said, "Remember, my father and I are two different people."

"I know that," Christina said. "I'm just . . . tonight's not good for me."

"I'll stop by the shop tomorrow," Andy said.

"Great," Christina told him, but she couldn't force herself to sound enthusiastic.

* * *

Christina biked home through the dark streets, cheered by the lights of Christmas trees in the houses. Some people had put electric candles in their windows. She especially liked those. They made her think of these houses in the past, before electricity, and how a candle in a window would cheer the person heading home through the dark.

She made a plan as she biked. She would not allow herself to obsess over Andy Bittlesman or over the rent hike. She'd keep herself busy making a stew, and maybe her mind, simmering on the back burner, so to speak, would surprise her with a solution.

Inside her house, she turned on the lights of her tree and sat admiring it for a few moments while Mittens curled in her lap purring loudly, glad Christina was home.

It was hard to be unhappy in the presence of an adoring cat and a beautiful Christmas tree, but the rent hike stabbed at her thoughts like a spear.

Ten percent? She would have to close her shop.

She went into the kitchen, prepared Mittens her evening feast, tied on an apron, and began putting together her stew. Somehow slicing carrots, potatoes, and parsnips was calming. She browned the stew meat, the minced garlic, and the chopped onions in olive oil, poured water and a good helping of red wine into the pot, covered it all, and let it simmer.

As she took off her apron, she felt much better.

The phone buzzed. Caller ID: Wink Lombard.

"Hi, sweetie," Christina said.

"Mom wants to know, can you come to dinner here tomorrow night?"

Christina was dumbfounded. She'd spoken only a few words to Delia the night of the tree decorating party. Would Oscar Bittlesman be there? Would Andy?

Whatever, Christina was not going to pass this up!

"I'd love to come, Wink. What time?"

"Mom says six-thirty."

"I'll see you then."

8

What do you wear to dinner at a billionaire's house?

What do you wear to dinner at an evil landlord's house?

The same thing you wear to dinner with a child you adore and a man you were on the verge of falling for until his father hiked the rent on your shop. Did Andy know about the rent hike? Did he care? Could he appreciate what the hike would mean for Christina and the other Shedders?

Could she mentally separate Andy from his father for this one night and enjoy being around the man who made her heart beat faster?

Be careful, her Inner Christina warned her.

Christina wore a formfitting dark green silk dress and a string of pearls. Janice Harris opened the door to her knock and said, "Welcome. Wow, Christina, you look fabulous."

"Thanks, Janice." It meant a lot to get the other woman's approval.

She was ushered into the living room where only a few days before she had helped put the Christmas tree in its stand. Now it was covered with very beautiful glass ornaments and, around the base, a few handmade Santas and snowflakes.

Oscar Bittlesman sat like a king in his throne in a dark leather chair near the fireplace. He wore a suit and tie and wing tips. Not the kind of guy to relax at home. Christina was glad she wore pearls.

"Christina!" Wink ran across the room to hug Christina. She wore a flouncy rainbow-colored party dress.

"You look so pretty!" Christina told Wink.

"You do, too." Wink held her hand and led her to a sofa.

"Hello, Christina." Delia wore white wool trousers and a white cashmere sweater.

"Christina." Andy nodded to her, smiling as if they shared a secret. He wore a navy blue sweater over his button-down shirt and tie.

What a bunch of stiffs! Christina thought.

"We're having prosecco," Delia said. "Except for Father, who's having Scotch. What would you like?"

"I'd like some prosecco, please." *Uh-oh,* Christina thought. *I'm turning into wood just like them!* Turning to Andy, she asked, "Did you have a good flight from New York?"

"It was bumpy," Andy told her. "I think the weather's changing."

Fortunately, that launched the group into a discussion about weather, which Christina thought would be a peaceful topic, and it was, until Wink announced that her former teacher was worried about global warming and climate change. Christina kept quiet, but watched with interest and admiration as Wink politely argued with her grandfather.

Christina studied Oscar Bittlesman. He was sixty-five (she'd googled) but looked a decade younger. He was slender and fit, and Christina clearly saw where his children and granddaughter got their looks. His blond hair had turned white. He kept it in a brush cut as if he was still in the military. (He'd been in the Marines; she'd googled.) When Andy or Delia quoted a fact about melting icebergs, Oscar waved it away. *Poppycock!*

Christina didn't know people even said *poppycock* these days. But when Wink quoted a fact, her grandfather listened and grudgingly said he was sure that was incorrect but he'd check it out.

Janice arrived to announce that dinner was ready. Following Oscar, they filed into the dining room, a large formal room with a seascape painted on the four walls. The table was beautifully set. Fresh flowers and candles in the middle. Shining silver utensils. White tablecloth and napkins. China plates in a pale green lavishly decorated with gold— Christina would have hung them on the wall.

"It's a simple family dinner tonight," Delia told her. "We won't have an appetizer."

"It smells divine," Christina told her.

The simple family dinner consisted of petite filet mignons for the women, much larger ones for the men, twice-baked potatoes, asparagus, and a small green salad. A red wine was served to everyone except Wink, who had milk. Everything was cooked to perfection, and everyone was glad to allow Wink to dominate the conversation so the rest of them could concentrate on the food.

Then Janice removed the plates. Oscar Bittlesman leaned back in his chair, patted his mouth with his stiff white linen napkin, and cleared his throat.

"You've lived here all your life, haven't you, Cheryl?"

Christina froze. Did he get her name wrong because he wanted to insult her? Or was he at the age where he simply had trouble remembering names? Would it be rude of her to correct him?

Wink saved the moment. "Oh, Grandfather, her name is Christina!" she told him, giggling.

"That's what I said!" Oscar Bittlesman retorted. He glared at Christina, as if *she'd* done something wrong.

"Yes," Christina replied. "I was born here, which makes me a native. I went off to Wheaton for college, and returned here when I got my degree."

"So you've never traveled."

"Actually, I have traveled. I've been to Europe with friends in college and to several states to visit friends." Oscar Bittlesman seemed intent on putting Christina in her place, whatever that place was. She wanted to derail this conversation. "I'm sure *you* have been *everywhere*," she said, gazing at the older man with intense admiration. And she did admire him. She knew he had accomplished a great deal in his life.

"Yes, actually, I have. I've been to Europe, of course, and Japan, China, India."

"Oh, dear, Christina," Delia cut in. "Now you've got him started. We'll be here all night."

Her father ignored her. "Australia and New Zealand, Iceland, and even Greenland."

"Have you been to Antarctica?" Christina's question sounded like a challenge, as if there was at least one place on the globe Oscar Bittlesman hadn't set foot.

Oscar smiled. Clearly he was enjoying this verbal jousting.

"Yes, actually, I have. I went on a National Geographic tour."

"And he saw penguins!" Wink interrupted enthusiastically. "Grandfather showed me pictures. Did you know there is a species of penguin called the macaroni penguin?"

Christina laughed. "I didn't know that. Why on earth would the bird be called that?"

Wink turned to Oscar. "You tell her, Grandfather. You know all the big words."

Oscar chuckled.

Oscar chuckled! Christina nearly fainted.

"The macaroni penguin is distinctive for the jaunty yellow crest it sports on top of its head. It got the name in the eighteenth century when the word 'macaroni' meant a flashy, flamboyant man."

"Like Elton John!" Wink said.

Christina burst out laughing at the thought of a penguin, Elton John–style. "How do you even know who Elton John is?"

"Oh, Mommy listens to him while she's exercising."

Delia cleared her throat. "All right, little missy. It's time for bed."

Wink pouted for a few seconds. Then she said, "Grandfather, may I please be excused from the table?"

"Of course," Oscar said. "Come give me a good-night kiss."

Wink jumped up, kissed her grandfather's cheek, and raced over to Christina.

"Thank you for coming!"

Christina hugged the little girl. "Thank you for inviting me."

"It's time for me to retire, as well," Oscar said, standing up.

Christina rose from the table. "Good night, Oscar, and thank you for inviting me."

Oscar flapped his hand, as if the evening meant nothing. "I'm sure we'll be talking again," he said, and just like that, he morphed from stiff but likeable curmudgeon to rapacious landlord.

Wink left the room, holding her mother's hand. Oscar followed.

"I have to go, too," Christina said.

"I wish I could drive you home," Andy told her as they went into the hall where Janice stood holding Christina's coat.

"I drove here myself," Christina reminded him. She wanted to kiss him good night, but Janice Harris was obviously determined to watch what happened next. "But I wish you could drive me home, too," she added in a softer voice, letting her eyes meet Andy's.

"I'll walk you to your car," Andy told her.

Christina smiled. She turned to Janice. "Thank you for the delicious meal, Janice."

"You're more than welcome," Janice said. "I hope I see you here again."

Janice's words made Christina feel warm and cozy, and then she stepped out onto the front porch.

It was raining.

"*Brrr!* If it's going to be this cold, we should at least have some snow!"

Andy took her hands in his. "I would love to keep you warm."

She smiled. "I'd like that, too."

"What did you think of Father?"

Christina took a moment to choose her words. "He's certainly impressive. Not quite as terrifying as I expected, and clearly he's got a soft spot for Wink."

"True. She's the apple of his eye." Andy pulled her close to him. "Can I see you tomorrow night?"

"I don't know. The store will be busy tomorrow." At the thought of the store, the knowledge of the rent hike hit her full force. "Andy . . . I have to tell you something. Just to clear the air."

"Okay."

Christina pulled away from him. "I don't want . . . oh, I'll just tell you. Your father has raised the rent on our sheds by ten percent, starting February first. I received a letter yesterday, and so did all the other Shedders."

"I didn't know that," Andy told her, speaking quietly. "That will be hard for you all, right?"

A streak of anger whipped through her. "Hard for us?

It'll mean we will no longer be able to continue renting the sheds." Christina turned her face, not wanting him to see the helpless tears rising in her eyes. "I'm going to have to close my shop."

"Christina, I had no idea. I'd offer to talk to my father, but right now I'm afraid that would do more harm than good. He's furious with me because I want to move to the island."

"I understand, Andy. And I don't want you to talk to him." Lifting her chin defiantly, Christina said, "I'm going to present my case to Oscar Bittlesman myself. I may be a small businesswoman, but I'm a good businesswoman." Her IC, who'd been quiet all through the dinner, cheered. *You go, girl!*

Reaching out, Andy put his hand against Christina's face and gently turned her so their eyes met. "Does that mean we can still see each other? Can I see you tomorrow night?"

Christina bowed her head. "Andy, you know I'm . . . attracted to you. But I don't think I can let myself feel any-thing—" She paused, trying to think of another word for *romantic*. "I mean, I don't want to get involved with you until I've at least tried to straighten things out with Oscar."

Andy laughed wryly. "All my life women have tried to attract me because they know my father's rich. You're the first woman who *won't* date me because my father's rich."

"It's not that, Andy," Christina said, moving away from his hand because it was very rapidly softening her heart and her brain and everything attached. "It's that I want to keep things clear between you and me."

"Okay, fine. Let's take one step at a time. Let me bring you dinner tomorrow night."

Christina studied Andy's face. They weren't even touching and she felt a profound connection to him that wasn't merely sexual, although, wow, was it sexual.

"I don't know," she said, her mood lightening. "Can you cook?"

Andy grinned. "I'll bring over my own special clam chowder."

"You make clam chowder?"

"I do. Matt Patterson showed me how this summer. It's got a few secret ingredients. I'll bring wine, too. And I'll pick up a baguette from the Wicked Island Bakery."

"You know Matt Patterson?" Christina asked. Matt was an island guy whose family had been on Nantucket for generations. He was a huge, cheerful, good-looking guy who hid his handsome face behind a beard he couldn't be bothered to cut and his body beneath Carhartt overalls that looked—and smelled—as if they'd never been washed. His hands were large and gnarly and scarred, and he'd lost the lobe of his left ear in a fight with a guy over a girl.

Andy grinned. "I do know Matt Patterson. Surprised, right? I'm not just another wealthy summer guy."

"I don't think you're like anyone else in the world," Christina told him. "Yes, please, bring me dinner tomorrow night."

Andy held his coat over Christina's head as they ran to her car. She hurriedly slid into the car's protection from the rain, waved at Andy, and drove away. She checked her rearview mirror. Andy was standing in the driveway, waving back.

* * *

She hadn't brought an umbrella with her, so when Christina reached her drive, she held her handbag over her head and raced to her door. By the time she got into the house, she was soaked.

Never before had she been so happy to see a Christmas tree in her living room, its small lights glowing on all the decorations. It was almost as good as having a friend there, welcoming her home, telling her to be of good cheer.

And that was a good thing, because her cat, curled up on the sofa, was totally unimpressed by Christina's return. Mittens had made a cozy bed out of the Christmas afghan. She looked warm and comfortable and utterly uninterested in Christina. When she heard Christina enter the room, she merely opened one eye, took notice of Christina, and closed her eye, returning to her snooze.

"Nice to see you, too, Mittens," Christina said sarcastically.

Christina shed her coat and shoes and dress in front of the door. She didn't want to drip water all through her house. She hurried to her bedroom, slipped on her warmest robe, and pulled a pair of wool socks onto her cold feet. She made herself a cup of hot cocoa with a marshmallow on top, sat down on the sofa near Mittens, and called Louise.

"Dora has the flu!" Louise complained. "And Karl has it, too. Dora didn't go to school and Karl didn't go to work. I've been waiting on them both hand and foot all day. I'm exhausted. Lord, I hope you didn't catch it from us."

"Oh, Louise, how can I help?"

"Really? I'd love it if you could get us some groceries: 7Up and chicken noodle soup and saltines and several pints of Ben & Jerry's for me."

"I'll go right now."

"I owe you big-time. Just put the bags on the porch. I don't want you breathing one atom from inside this house."

"Do you need aspirin?"

"No, but thank heavens you asked, we're almost out of Children's Tylenol."

"I'll get that, too."

"You're an angel."

Christina got dressed again, in sweatpants and a sweat-shirt this time, and pulled on an ancient wool hat her mother had knitted her years ago.

The parking lot at the supermarket was crowded. Here were all the people who worked all day and had to do their shopping in the evening. As Christina pushed her rattling cart (why did *she* always get the cart with the squeaky, wonky wheel?) through the aisles, she stopped to chat with so many of her friends and acquaintances.

"Oh, poor Dora," Susan Waters said. "I'll make a big pan of lasagna and take it over to Louise tomorrow."

"I've heard that flu is going around," Tim Randolph said. "We bought some kid DVDs about a month ago and we've watched them so much we can say the words with the characters. I'll put a pile together and drop them by their house tomorrow."

"Half the school is out with the flu," Anna Jane Butler told Christina. "It's not a huge problem. We go on recess for Christmas at the end of next week."

"Here," Alison Price said as she dug around in her enormous leather bag. "I just finished this book and it's fabulous! Fast plot, gorgeous men, and plenty of steam. When you take Dora the groceries, drop this off for Louise."

When she returned to her Jeep, Christina scarcely noticed the cold air. The brightly lit displays of reindeer and snowmen and Santas in people's yards cheered her, and she was warmed all through from seeing so many generous friends. She hoped someday she'd have a child with the flu. A short-lived, mild flu, of course. And a husband who had the flu, too. She could imagine Wink as her child, but she couldn't fit Andy into the husband slot.

She carried the two bags of goodies to Louise's front porch and talked to her on her cell as she drove home. (She knew she shouldn't talk and drive, but her cell synced to her radio so she could drive with both hands.) She told Louise about the DVDs from Tim Randolph and the book from Alison Price and the lasagna Susan Waters would bring over the next day.

"Gosh, this is so nice it makes me want to cry," Louise said. "And I haven't even asked you how your day was."

Christina didn't want to download all her worries on Louise, not tonight when Louise had a house full of sick people. "Let's just say it was complicated. I'll give you the details when we can get together for a glass of wine. Or maybe a few shots of tequila."

They laughed together, said goodbye, and Christina clicked off. Seeing her friends in the grocery store had lifted her mood, and she'd bought herself an entire box of Ferrero Rocher (she wouldn't eat them *all* tonight) and some gourmet cat treats for Mittens. She shed her raincoat and wool cap and shoes at the front door, pulled on her pajamas and cozy robe, set the half-empty cup of hot chocolate in the sink, and her box of chocolates on the sofa. Before she sat down, she had to do one more thing.

"Here, Mittens," she said in her sweetest voice. "I brought you a present."

Mittens was sulking under the dining room table. She heard Christina rip open the foil package. Christina made a wavy path of cat treats across the floor and up onto the sofa where she settled with the TV remote in her hand. Mittens approached Christina warily, as if Christina were some kind of shape-shifter. The smell of duck liver must have been irresistible, because Mittens ate them all. The cat curled in Christina's lap exactly when Christina clicked the remote to the Hallmark Channel, the one definite location where true love existed.

9

That night, on the mainland, in Boston and on the Cape, snow fell, icing the homes and stores and roads and bridges with sparkling white.

On Nantucket Island, thirty miles from the mainland, it rained.

And rained.

Christina phoned to tell Wink not to come to work today. It wouldn't be busy, not with all the rain.

A few customers slogged through the wet streets to the shops, not bothering to carry umbrellas because the wind would turn them inside out. People hated the rain, and frankly, so did Christina. Every time her door opened, a minor tsunami blew into her shop. Her customers dripped water on the floor. When they picked up an object, water dribbled from their shoulders and rain hats onto the merchandise, the boxes of Legos, the fancy mermaids, the books, the puzzles, the whales.

The little sheds shuddered with the impact of the wind.

When people asked if the place was safe, Christina assured them the sheds had stood for over a hundred years.

Still, it was cold in her shop in spite of her space heater turned to high. Customers didn't linger. She didn't blame them.

Lunch at Mimi's was marginally better. Her shed trembled in the high wind, but she had three space heaters. The group gathered around the one in the back of the store and were thrilled to eat their food with their gloves off.

"Okay," Harriet said, "we're all here, and I'm calling this meeting to order. First item of business—Christina. Spill."

Christina took a bite of her sandwich. Today she had peanut butter and jelly, an inexpensive and easy food, but the peanut butter stuck to her teeth. She looked over at beautiful Harriet in her cashmere shawl pinned at the shoulder with a ruby and gold sleigh.

"So I went to dinner," she managed to say. She took a sip of water. "I met the great man himself, Oscar Bittlesman. The dining room was so elegant, and Janice Harris served filet mignons. Delia was there, and Wink and Andy, and it was all pleasant enough, even though Oscar called me *Cheryl* and went on to express the opinion that I probably had never traveled."

Mimi leaned forward. "Was he trying to insult you by calling you *Cheryl*?"

Christina thought about it. "I don't think so. I think it was just a slip of the tongue."

"He's over sixty-five," Mimi reminded her. "Believe me, by then it's often hard to remember your dog's name."

"Did you talk about the rent?" Jacob asked.

"No. He didn't bring it up and neither did I. It wasn't the appropriate time or place. But I will make an appointment to speak to him. I'm not as afraid of him as I was, probably because I can tell he's got such a soft spot for Wink."

"And does Andy have a soft spot for you?" Harriet inquired, a snide tone to her voice and a taunting look on her face.

Christina hadn't planned on telling Harriet or anyone, but she couldn't resist replying, "He might."

"Lucky you," Harriet said sadly. Rallying, she turned to Jacob. "And you, Jacob, spent a lot of time at Christina's party talking to Delia Bittlesman. What were you talking about?"

Jacob shrugged. "I went to school with a friend of hers."

"What school?" Harriet asked.

"Just high school."

Harriet leaned forward, peering at him intensely. "What is it you aren't telling us? I'll bet it was a boarding school!"

Jacob raised his head. "You're making too much of this. It was St. Mark's, that's all."

Harriet sat back, surprised. After a moment, she asked, "Jacob, are you rich?"

"Harriet!" Mimi scolded. Like a teacher with a child, she instructed, "Jacob, you don't have to answer that. Harriet, stop it."

Harriet's shoulders sagged. "I apologize. It's just this rent hike that's making me crazy."

"We're all crazy because of it," Christina reminded her.

"Hey, heads up! Customers headed our way," Mimi said.

"I'll finish my lunch in my shop," Christina said.

Jacob and Harriet agreed, and they all rushed back with rain pelting down on them.

The rest of the afternoon dragged. Few customers braved the torrential rain, and everyone commented that they wished it would snow. At six o'clock on the dot, Christina shut and locked her shop door and ran through the puddles to her car.

At home, Christina fed the cat, plugged in the lights of the Christmas tree, took a shower, and wondered what she should wear tonight. Something comfortable, cozy, and kind of sexy. Something to wear while eating clam chowder that subtly hinted: *Kiss me*. Nothing in her wardrobe fit that particular category, so she settled for skinny jeans and a loose cashmere pullover.

She set the table for two, prepared a green salad, and put a bottle of white wine in the refrigerator to chill. The rain had finally ended, but outside the night was dark and the air was chilly. She lit candles on the table and around the room.

Andy knocked. She hurried to open the door.

"I've brought dinner," Andy told her, nodding toward

the large covered pot he held, a Wicked Island Bakery baguette carefully balanced along the top.

"Bring it in!" Christina led him to the kitchen.

Andy set the pot on the stove, turned the heat to low, and lifted the lid. A mouthwatering aroma filled the air.

"That smells amazing," Christina told Andy.

And then she looked at him, really looked at him, with his blue eyes and his sweet mouth.

She said, "Hello."

"Hello," he said.

Leaning over, he kissed her softly, briefly on her lips.

Stepping back, Andy said, "The chowder's almost ready. I need to add this pint of cream and then we just have to warm it up."

"Want a glass of white wine while you work?"

"Sure."

"I've made a salad," Christina said.

"Perfect."

Andy stirred the chowder, Christina added the finishing touches to their dinner, and Mittens came sauntering in, waving her tail and weaving around Andy's ankles.

"Hang on, beauty queen. I'll fish out a few clams for you in a minute."

Mittens purred, as if she understood.

When Mittens was satisfied and the room was warm and fragrant, Christina and Andy settled at the kitchen table, their chowder steaming from deep bowls. For a while, they only ate, and the chowder was so rich and delicious, Christina nearly purred herself.

She sat back in her chair and sipped her wine. "How's

Wink? I called and told her not to come in today because business would be so slow."

"Good thing. Delia thinks she's coming down with a cold and kept her in bed all day. She even allowed her to watch TV and videos on her phone. I think Oscar played a game of checkers with her."

"I'm glad your father's such a good grandfather."

"At this time in her life, she needs all the good males around her she can get. She's been pretty much abandoned by her father. She can't afford to dislike her grandfather."

"I understand."

"I think you've been a good influence on her, Christina," Andy said.

"I hope so. She learns fast. She's become a real help in the shop. But more than that, she's just a darling little girl." Her heart swelled with love for Wink. *Silly Christina*, she thought, quickly looking down.

Andy continued, "I wonder if she isn't also influenced . . . to be honest, I think I mean *enchanted* by this island. I mean, this town is absolutely the size for a child to grasp. It's like a story. The butcher, the baker, the candlestick maker. The Christmas trees and the lights turn this into a fairy tale. I think Wink is happier than she's been in her young life."

"I'm glad. I agree, the town can often enchant people. But, Andy, what's going to happen when she returns to New York?"

"She'll be able to come here for summers and holidays. Delia and Wink can stay at our father's house."

As they finished their meals, Christina said, "The rain has really stopped."

"Good. I'd like to take a walk. I think I ate too much."

"It's your own fault. That clam chowder was crazy good." She'd enjoy walking in the clear, cold air, too, Christina thought. "Andy, want to go somewhere fun? I mean, the Brant Point lighthouse, the short, fat lighthouse right on the curve of beach entering into the harbor. Have you been there before? Has Wink?"

Andy laughed at her enthusiasm. "I don't know about Wink, but I haven't."

"Good. Get your coat. We're going for a little adventure."

They quickly stacked the dishes in the dishwasher and tidied the kitchen in case Mittens felt like exploring. They pulled on their warm coats, wool hats, thick gloves.

"We'll take my car," Christina said. "I know where we're going."

"Fine," Andy agreed, sliding into the passenger seat.

Christina drove her car down the quiet streets from town, past the yacht club and the White Elephant hotel and a row of waterfront mansions until they came to the end of the road and the beginning of the beach.

"Take off your shoes and socks," Christina said. "You don't want sand in your shoes."

"Well, I don't want cold feet!" Andy responded.

"Silly, it's not that cold." She whisked off her shoes and jumped out of the car. "Hurry!"

She ran. For a few steps, her feet touched tarmac, and then she was on the beach, running toward the Brant Point lighthouse. She veered around it and raced down to the edge of the water. When Andy caught up with her, she tugged his arm and pointed.

"Look."

Above them, the clouds were fading from the night sky. Stars came out, twinkling in the dark. Across the harbor, no lights shone—most houses along the harbor front were summer houses. Behind them, the lights of town beamed, but right here at this point, the sky and water were dark.

Then, through the darkness, came the Hy-Line ferry, moving smoothly, even regally, through the waters. From the many passenger windows and the pilothouse, dozens of lights shone, the nautical lights and the colorful Christmas lights strung around the boat. For a few moments, it was as if creatures made of light were headed toward them, and then the ferry moved closer, its engines rumbling as it slowed down for harbor waters, and the lights became brighter, and through the foggy windows shapes and colors moved as people gathered their belongings and got ready to disembark. Soon the large ship was beside the lighthouse and it seemed as big as a castle. Slowly, it turned toward the docking area and slid away.

"That was breathtaking," Andy said.

Christina stepped closer to him, leaning into him as he put his arm around her. "I know. We seldom take the time to watch the ferries arrive in the dark. It happens every day, but if you're here at the right time, it's kind of mysterious, isn't it? Kind of magical."

"You're kind of magical," Andy said, and bent his face to hers and kissed her.

Christina stood on her tiptoes to reach his mouth. She wrapped her arms around his neck. Andy cupped his hand on the back of her head and gently pressed her to him. They kissed for a long time, leaning into each other, and while Christina was sexually aroused—she'd take off her clothes and let him have her right here on the cold sand if he asked her—she was also aware of a sense of promise in their kiss, a silent pledge for their future.

When they stepped back from one another, Christina felt the magical glow had entered her heart. "There are so many places on the island I'd love to show you."

"And I want to see them all. With you. But I do have a problem."

Her heart lurched. That kiss had been so *serious*. Andy had meant something with that kiss. And now he was going to tear apart the lovely spell they were in? Her voice cracked when she said, "Okay. Tell me."

"My feet are freezing. Could we please go back to our shoes?"

Christina burst out laughing. "Of course! But first I want to show you one more thing."

Taking him by the hand, she pulled him around the corner of Brant Point and gestured up toward the fat little Brant Point lighthouse. "The Coast Guard hangs this every year. It takes several men to secure it."

"That's the biggest Christmas wreath I've ever seen," Andy said.

"You've got your tree at Rockefeller Center, we've got our Christmas wreath," Christina joked.

"It's beautiful," Andy said. "And I can no longer feel my toes."

Christina laughed again. "I'll race you to the car."

They reached her car and perched on the edge of the seats to brush the sand off their feet. They put on their shoes, settled in the car, and Christina punched the ignition, turning the heat to high.

They looked at each other and smiled and couldn't look away.

Andy took her hand. "I have to go to New York for business tomorrow. I'll be gone two or three days. I'd like to see you when I get back to the island."

Christina smiled. "Call me when you know your flight number. I'll pick you up at the airport. Unless you want to come on the ferry at night."

"I'll call you either way." Andy took a deep breath. "Christina, I really like you. It's probably a good thing I'm going away. You and I need to catch our breath. I don't want to, but I'm old enough now to understand I shouldn't go all adolescent over you."

Christina laughed. "Oh, *please* go all adolescent over me!"

In response, he pulled her to him and kissed her for a long time. When he released her, he said, "Consider that a sample."

She looked away, not wanting him to see how very much he moved her, how his kiss had meant more than she'd ever experienced, how euphoric she felt—and how vulnerable. Andy was, after all, Oscar Bittlesman's son. He lived in New York, he had money, he could have any woman he wanted, and he probably intended to marry a woman of his own set, a wealthy woman who owned diamonds and would run international charities and use nannies for her children. A woman who was a model, like the exotically beautiful Anastasiya Belousova.

Christina had never felt more serious about a man in her life, and she'd never believed so surely that she was headed for heartbreak.

"Christina? Are you okay?"

She turned to face him. She softly ran her fingertips along the side of his face, and then, tenderly, over his lips.

"I'm fine, Andy. More than fine. But I should go home. I've got a busy day tomorrow."

"Of course."

At her house, Andy walked her to the front door. He bent to kiss her sweetly, briefly, politely.

"I'll call you from New York. As often as I can."

"I'll be waiting."

10

Christina woke early with a smile on her face.

"Oh, stop it!" she ordered her bewitched brain. "No thinking about Andy Bittlesman today. You have work to do."

She threw back the covers, which accidentally landed on Mittens, causing the poor cat to jump two feet in the air.

"I'm sorry, Mittens," Christina said. She took a few minutes to cuddle her cat, who had been ignored recently and also shut in the kitchen during the day so she couldn't smack all the ornaments off the Christmas tree.

She showered, dressed, ate a bowl of hot oatmeal, and filled her go-cup with coffee. She checked the weather report on her phone. No snow predicted, but no rain, either. She wheeled her bike from the garage and headed into town.

Business was brisk and Christina was in a great mood when she went to Mimi's to have lunch with the others.

She was surprised, once she settled in the back room, at the way everyone was staring at her expectantly.

"What have I done?" she asked, unwrapping her peanut butter and jelly sandwich, her fastest, easiest lunch sandwich, which would be her standby until after Christmas.

"That's what we want to know!" Harriet snapped. "You had a date with Andy Bittlesman last night."

"What Harriet would like to know, as would we all," Mimi softly refereed, "is whether you were able to convince him to keep his father from raising the rents."

For a moment, Christina couldn't speak. Literally. The peanut butter was sticking her mouth shut. She took the moment to consider her answer.

"We didn't talk about his father or the rent hikes," Christina admitted. "It simply wasn't the right time."

"What, you can't talk about money at your house?" Harriet demanded.

Christina's jaw dropped. "Wait. What? How did you know where we ate?"

"Oh, come on, Christina. It's a small town. Andy Bittlesman is big gossip. Word gets around."

Christina waited to hear whether or not someone saw them kissing at Brant Point. But it was Jacob who spoke up.

"Christina, please forgive us for prying into your affairs. But you know we're all worried about that rent hike. I think we're more anxious than usual."

Jacob was such a sweet, courteous man. Christina felt awful, as if she had failed him, and the others, by not pushing about the rent hike.

"I know you are," Christina said. "I am, too. I'm just trying to be diplomatic about it."

"We don't have much more time, you know," Mimi

said. "It's the middle of December. After Christmas, we'll have a brief rush when people spend their Christmas money, and then January will be a vast frozen wasteland."

"And the lights will be off in our shops," Harriet said bitterly.

"I've been talking with a real estate dealer, a friend of mine," Jacob said. "I was hoping to find someplace else in town where we could have our shops. So far, nothing. This island is becoming so popular, every square inch of space in the town is priceless."

Mimi started to cry. "I've had my shop here for thirty years!"

"You," Harriet almost snarled at Christina, "will probably marry the rich guy and forget all about us."

Christina was shocked. Harriet and Jacob were desperate, and beloved Mimi was *crying*. Really, what had she been thinking? She hadn't been thinking, she'd been caught up in a dream world where she could marry the man she loved. The truth was she was a shopkeeper, only able to run her shop because she'd inherited a house on the island and didn't have to pay rent or mortgage. Andy was like a glamorous fantasy, but of course they wouldn't last, while Mimi, Jacob, and even Harriet had been her buddies for years. She wouldn't desert them.

"I'm sorry I disappointed you all," she said. "I'm worried, too. Here's what I'll do. I'm going to call and ask for a private appointment with Oscar Bittlesman. I'll state my case logically, and I'll present it as fiercely and firmly as I can. I'll let you know what happens."

Mimi began to hum the theme song from *Rocky*.

Harriet raised her two arms in the air. "Go, Christina! You're our hero."

Jacob said, "She's our heroine."

Christina smiled and said, "You all had better wait and see."

Wink arrived at the shop for her "job" at exactly one o'clock. Several customers had asked to have their purchases gift wrapped, and after Christina showed Wink how to wrap the presents neatly, Wink tucked into a space in the corner and worked away. She was tidy and careful and efficient.

When the shop was empty, Christina told Wink about the Christmas movies coming to the Dreamland. As they moved around setting the shelves in order, they felt the wind rise. Waves sloshed around beneath the wharf and even with the space heater, the interior of the shop was chilly.

Just before dark, Wink raced over to the public restroom on the north side of the wharf.

"Christina, I almost fell into the harbor!" Wink announced as she returned to the shop. "The bathroom door is so close to the water."

Christina knelt and wrapped her arms around Wink. "Oh, dear, are you all right?"

"Oh, I'm okay. I just got scared."

"The other shopkeepers and I have to have that changed. Maybe we can concentrate on that after the first of the year." Christina started to say more—she started to say, *Tell your grandfather that you almost fell into the water!* That might make him understand Christina's point of view—true, their sheds were quaint, but the facilities needed improving. But she knew it wouldn't be right to use Wink as a pawn in her battle with Oscar.

A mother and daughter entered the shop just then, and Christina and Wink went back to work. At four, Wink skipped down to Main Street where Janice was waiting to drive her home.

Light faded from the sky. Fewer people came into Christina's shop. It was bitterly cold outside. Christina was determined to stay open until six, because she usually had a few customers who raced in, bought something at the end of the day, and raced away. But now, for the few minutes she was alone, she decided to make a phone call.

She found the landline number in the phone book. She dialed.

A woman answered, very formally. "Bittlesman residence."

"Hi, Janice. It's me, Christina. Could I speak with Mr. Bittlesman, please?"

"Oh, honey, he left the island this morning."

"Oh! No, wait, I mean old Mr. Bittlesman. Oh, dear, don't tell him I said *old.* I meant Mr. Bittlesman senior."

"I'll see if he's available. Hold on, please."

Christina waited patiently, and finally Oscar's strong and crusty voice came on the line.

"Hello, Christina. I didn't expect to hear from you again."

"Oscar, Mr. Bittlesman, could I come talk with you some day soon? I won't take much of your time." She hated herself for her ingratiating tone. She wasn't a child and he wasn't the elementary school principal. But her responsibility to the other Shedders and her need to keep her shop open gave her courage.

Oscar was quiet for such a long time, Christina wondered if he'd fallen asleep.

"Day after tomorrow!" he barked. "Six o'clock. My house. We'll have a drink."

"Wonderful! I'll be there."

At lunch the next day, as they gathered in Mimi's back room, Christina told them about her plan.

"Well done!" Mimi said.

"Wait, I haven't done anything yet."

"You absolutely have! Bearding the lion in his den! Talking to him man-to-man instead of using your friendship with Wink or with Andy to support you. Don't try to sugarcoat it. Tell him in no uncertain terms a ten percent raise is not acceptable."

"And don't wear that!" Harriet cut in.

Christina blinked, surprised at Harriet's bossy tone. She looked down at her outfit. Corduroy trousers tucked into Ugg boots, a red sweater, a bright green inexpensive shell necklace she sold in the store.

"Why not?" Christina asked. "I look Christmasy."

"You look cute. You need to look businesslike. You need to seem totally grown up."

Mimi nodded. "Harriet's right. You've got to be large and in charge."

"Maybe one of you should come with me. Maybe you, Harriet. You're more this type."

Harriet actually blushed. "No, thank you. I'd just be a distraction."

"Fine," Christina said. "I'll let you know how it goes."

That night she did everything she could to keep herself calm, to not dwell on what to wear tomorrow night, what to say. She built a fire, made hot cocoa with a marshmallow in it, and put on some low-key Christmas music. If she let herself think about it, she was sorry she had to face Oscar Bittlesman alone. Really, the other three Shedders should go with her. A group of four would be more persuasive than one.

Her phone buzzed. Christina's heart leapt.

It was Andy.

"How was your day?" she asked.

"Endless. Boring. Nerve-wracking. There are times when I think my colleagues are being obtuse just to drive me mad."

Christina laughed. "My colleague is much nicer. She's funny and quick and loves her work."

Andy chuckled. "She's very happy there. She really likes Dora. They're having a sleepover next Saturday night. Before that, Dora's mom is taking the girls to the ice skating rink. And Sunday, they're going to the high school pool for open swim time."

"Lucky girl. And that reminds me, the Theatre Workshop of Nantucket is running *Miracle on 34th Street*. We might want to go and take Wink."

"Or we might want Delia to take Wink, and you and I could see a grown-up play."

Christina laughed. "Actually, I love *Miracle on 34th Street*. But I'll check and see what's on at the White Heron. Oh! Dreamland Theater is streaming a live production of the Bolshoi Ballet doing *The Nutcracker*. One afternoon only."

Andy paused. "Mmm, you know I can see ballet live, here in the city. Some opera, too."

Defensively, Christina said, "It's true, we don't have the cultural variety you have in the city, but we have things on the island that make up for that."

"Sorry, Christina, I didn't mean to sound like a jerk."

"I know you didn't. I know better than anyone how quiet it gets here in the winter. But somehow we've all found our own special pleasures—book clubs, bridge, visiting lecturers . . . Oh! I almost forgot. I'm invited for a drink at your father's house tomorrow night."

"Get out of town."

"It's true. I called and asked to meet him and we're set for tomorrow evening. Drinks. At his house."

"Good luck," Andy said.

"Thank you. I know I'll need it."

"You've seen the man in his civil persona. You're about to meet him as his true self, a businessman with no heart of gold. I would be amazed if he changed his mind."

"I'd hate myself if I didn't try," Christina told him.

"Whatever happens, will you call me afterward and tell me about it?"

"Of course, if you want me to."

"I want you to. And, Christina, remember: I'm on your side."

"Thank you, Andy. That means a lot to me."

"You mean a lot to me," Andy told her.

Christina fell asleep with stars in her eyes after her conversation with Andy, but she woke with butterflies in her stomach, thinking of Oscar. She took a long time getting dressed, wanting to look warm and welcoming to her customers, but businesslike and competent to Oscar.

Her morning in the shop flew by. Snow was forecast for the next day, and people were rushing around buying presents now while the streets were dry.

At noon, she headed down the wharf for lunch at Mimi's. The other three were already there.

"We shouldn't stay long," Jacob said. "Today's a good shopping day and we don't want to lose customers."

"We don't have to stay at all," Christina said. "I've often eaten my lunch while working." She hadn't taken off her gloves, so she waved and turned to go.

"Wait, Christina!" Mimi called. "Wait a moment. We can take a few minutes. Sit down. All of you, sit down."

Puzzled, Christina sat.

"Christina," Mimi said seriously, "we want you to know we're aware of what a burden we're placing on you, asking you to make Oscar change his mind. We can't be with you in body—I believe he'll be much more receptive to you than he would be to the gang of us. But we want to give you something to take with you so you'll know we're there with you in spirit."

Mimi handed Christina a small velvet box. Christina opened it to find a gold snowflake on a chain. "Mimi! You didn't have to do this."

"Wouldn't have done it if I'd had to." Mimi chuckled. "Here, let me fasten it around your neck."

"And I'm giving you my uncle's ancient briefcase." Jacob brought out a handsome, scuffed leather briefcase. "You can carry it into the meeting with Oscar this evening looking professional. You won't look like someone who deals in stuffed bunnies. You'll look like a businesswoman who can do her own taxes and knows the value of a dollar."

Tears flooded Christina's eyes. "This is a wonderful gift, Jacob. Thank you. I'm going to feel powerful and proud with this in my hand."

"Harriet?" Mimi prodded.

Harriet could scarcely look away from the briefcase. Almost grudgingly, she said, "Okay, Christina. Here's my offering. It's a vintage Hermès scarf. Worth a fortune. Actually, it will go well with what you're wearing." She rose, tied the scarf around Christina's neck, and adjusted it so that it hung perfectly.

"Thank you, Harriet," Christina said.

"You're welcome—strings are attached. If you get him to keep the rent stable, you can keep it. If you fail, I get it back."

Christina burst out laughing. "Agreed!" She looked

from person to person. "Thank you all. These will be my good luck charms."

"Let us know what happens," Mimi said.

"I will. I promise."

The group broke up to return to their shops, which was a good thing, because it seemed everyone in town was shopping.

11

Christina closed her shop and hurried down to her car, parked on the bottom of Main Street. She'd taken care with her clothes that morning, wearing a navy blue pantsuit that she thought made her look professional, the owner of a viable business, not just a young woman playing with toys. Now with the briefcase, the gold charm, and the Hermès scarf, Christina felt two inches taller and fifty IQ points smarter. She was good to go!

While her car warmed up, she pulled off the Uggs that had kept her feet warm all day and put on a pair of low-heeled shoes. She freshened her lipstick and mascara. She stared at her reflection in the rearview mirror and said, "Good luck."

Janice welcomed her at the door and escorted her to Oscar's library. At first, Christina was so stunned, she couldn't remember why she was here. All those books! And the flickering fire and the plump, inviting leather chairs!

"Oh, my goodness," Christina said. "This room is heaven! I could stay here forever!"

Oscar was sitting behind a massive desk, shuffling through papers. "Yes," Oscar said. "I like it."

His businesslike tone brought Christina to her senses. She regretted having spoken so impulsively. She switched into her efficient, professional mode.

"Oscar, Mr. Bittlesman, I'd like to talk with you about—"

"What's your poison?" he demanded.

"What?"

Oscar's mouth twitched in amusement. "I asked you what you would like to drink. I prefer Scotch."

"I'd like a glass of wine. Red or white, whatever is easiest. Or prosecco, but you probably don't have that. I can have Scotch." Christina wanted to clamp her mouth shut with her hands to stop her nervous blathering.

Oscar shot her a sour look. He pressed an intercom. "Janice, I'd like my Scotch now, please. And Miss Antonioni would like a glass of wine. She doesn't know what kind she likes, so I'll let you decide for her."

Oh, Lord, Christina thought.

He gestured to a small sofa. "Sit down."

Christina sat. Oscar continued to work on his papers, so Christina waited patiently, hoping to keep in the man's good graces.

Janice entered with two glasses on a tray. She took a glass of white wine to Christina and a beautiful Waterford tumbler half-filled with amber liquid to Oscar. She left the room quietly.

"Cheers," Oscar said, raising his glass.

"Cheers!" Christina replied, suddenly hopeful that this change in Oscar would predict a good meeting.

"Now. What did you come to talk about?" Oscar asked.

Before she could answer, the door flew open and Wink zoomed in.

"Christina! I didn't know you were here."

"I'm here for a business talk," Christina told the little girl.

"Oh, good!" Wink looked at her grandfather. "I'm learning all about business!"

"In that case," Oscar said, "you may stay here as long as you keep quiet. This conversation is between adults."

Wink perched on a chair, folded her hands in her lap, and solemnly nodded.

Christina cleared her throat. "I'm here, Oscar, Mr. Bittlesman, on behalf of the four of us who run businesses on Straight Wharf. I know you've lived on the island for a few years, so I'm sure you know how the time of year affects our businesses. We make most of our money in the summer months. And during Christmas. We don't make a large income from our shops, just barely enough to keep going, actually." She reached into her handsome briefcase and brought out a folder. Leaning forward, she set it on his desk. "These are my tax statements for the past two years. I also brought the figures for Mimi's Seaside Souvenirs. You can see that we can barely cover utilities and also make a small salary. If you raise the rent on the sheds, we'll have to go out of business."

She paused. She had done the best she could, and she thought she had spoken succinctly and calmly, even though beneath her business suit, her heart was dancing the flamenco.

Oscar flipped through her folder. Then he shrugged.

"I have business expenses, also," Oscar said. "I am, after all, a businessman. Have you ever thought that perhaps your businesses per se aren't worth the trouble of running? *I'm* not to blame for that. I'm sure that if you four close shop, our firm will be able to find other people, with more attractive products, to take over."

Christina took a deep breath. She'd written out this little speech the night before and memorized it.

"Oscar, what possible good could you achieve if you get rid of us? Maybe you could make ten percent more with other merchants. But Nantucket has always been about community. We know we're isolated here thirty miles offshore. So we help each other. We don't want to get rich at the expense of our neighbors."

"Miss Antonioni."

She ignored his interruption. She was determined to say her piece. "And have you ever been in any of the shops? Did you ever personally come into Christina's Toy Shop to choose a toy for Wink? Have you ever bought an anemometer? Part of living on the island is preparing for gale-force winds. Have you ever bought a kite and taken Wink to fly it on the beach? And how charming would it be if you wore a sweatshirt with Santa riding a whale on it on Christmas Day? You could have so much more fun doing any of those things than sitting here barricaded in your house."

"Miss Antonioni." Oscar's words were a warning.

Christina persisted. "You should come have lunch with the Shedders, get to know us a bit. Mimi is the most adorable, generous woman on the island. She would probably *give* you a sweatshirt, and she would definitely make you laugh. And you could stop in at the Hy-Line office. Many of the clerks there grew up on the island and they know the history. You could learn all about Nantucket. If you—"

"*Miss Antonioni!*" Oscar rose from the desk, his fists pushing into the blotter, his head shoved forward.

He looked, Christina thought, much like a gorilla ready to charge. *Oh, dear,* she thought, *this can't be good.*

"I don't care about all your cute little friends. I didn't get rich by playing games with cute little friends. I'm a businessman. *I don't want your friendship. I want your money.*"

Christina's mouthed gaped in shock. She'd never heard anyone say that before, not even the real estate dealers.

She desperately tried to think of something to say.

Then Wink rose from her chair with her small hands wrapped around each other and her blue eyes as wide as saucers and her face all scrunched up in worry. "But, Grandfather! Why do you care about money? You *have* money. You don't have any *friends*. You need friends."

Oscar's face turned burgundy. He yelled at Wink, "Get out of my house!"

Wink burst into tears and ran from the room. A moment later, the front door slammed.

Christina stood up, alarmed and angry. "How can you tell your granddaughter to leave your house?"

"I didn't say that!" Oscar bellowed. "I told her to get out of the room."

"No, Mr. Bittlesman, you told her to leave your *house*. That's why you heard the front door slam." A vein was throbbing on Oscar's forehead. Christina didn't want the older man to have a stroke.

Oscar sank back into his cushy leather chair. He reached for his Scotch and drank it all in one gulp. His hands were shaking.

"I'm sorry if I caused such a disturbance," Christina said. "I'll leave now. And see if I can find Wink."

Christina stepped into the large front hall and began the exhausting process of pulling on her parka, her gloves, her hat, her scarf.

Janice came into the hall. "Is everything all right?"

Christina was trembling and worried and angry and sick at heart. "Oh, sure, everything's just fine. Mr. Bittlesman told his granddaughter to leave his house, and she ran out and I'm not certain she's wearing a coat and Mr. Bittlesman is about to have a heart attack and I'll have to close my shop on February first and so will my wharf friends."

Janice took Christina's hands in hers. "Sweetheart, Mr. Bittlesman almost has a heart attack every day. Also, he's getting older, and he often uses the wrong word. I'm positive he meant for Wink to get out of the room, not his house. Wink is a smart girl. She'll understand that when she cools down."

"Well," Christina said, nodding toward the fleecy pink jacket that Wink always wore. "I'm sure she's cooling down now. Thank you, Janice. I feel calmer now. I'm going to go find Wink."

"Call me when you find her and I'll call you if she comes home."

"Thanks." Christina pulled on her gloves and hurried out the door.

* * *

Because most of the houses on the cliff were summer houses, few lights illuminated the dark. Christina had a flashlight on her phone. Using it, she slowly walked around the Bittlesmans' house, in case Wink was hiding behind a bush. But she found no one.

It was exceptionally cold. By all logic, it should be snowing now, but the sky was clear. Christina slid into her old Jeep and turned on the ignition and the heat. She sat a moment, letting the car warm up and gathering her thoughts.

Her phone buzzed. Without checking the caller ID, Christina answered.

"I am going to sue you until you don't have a pair of shoes to wear!"

"Delia?"

"Yes, of course it's me. My father just told me that you made my daughter run away from home and Wink has *never* done that before! I can't *believe*—"

"Delia, I know you're upset, and I'd like to talk with you about this but right now I've got to concentrate on Wink. I'll find her, I promise."

"Call me the moment you do."

"I will."

"Oh, Wink," Christina moaned as she tucked the phone in her coat pocket, "where are you? You must be freezing."

"I am!"

Christina shrieked.

Wink giggled and unfolded her small self from the floor of the backseat.

"Wink, you almost gave me a heart attack," Christina scolded.

Immediately Wink looked contrite. "I'm sorry, Christina. But I am cold."

"Come up here and cuddle with me for a moment and then I'll take you in to your grandfather."

Like a little pink eel, Wink easily slithered up and over the back of the passenger seat. She couldn't properly cuddle with the gear shift in the way, so she climbed onto Christina's lap and snuggled up there like a kitten. Christina pulled her own coat around her.

"Grandfather's mad at me," Wink said, squirming to get comfortable and inadvertently elbowing Christina in the ribs.

"Your grandfather is mad at *me*," Christina said. "We were having a business meeting and those can often become confrontational. We shouldn't have let you remain in the room."

"Grandfather gets mad a lot."

"Look," Christina said, shifting around to keep her leg from falling asleep, "before we do anything else, you need to call your mother and tell her you're okay."

Wink looked glum. "She'll be mad."

"She's your mother. You disappeared. Of course she'll be mad."

With a theatrical sigh, Wink took Christina's phone and called her mother. The conversation was loud.

"But he *did* say it, Mommy! Grandfather told me to get out of his house. He really said that. He did! Ask Christina." After another few minutes of listening to her mother, Wink said, "Okay" and handed the phone to Christina.

"Take my daughter into the house *right* now," Delia ordered. "You've caused enough uproar in our family already."

Christina opened her mouth to object but changed her mind. Delia was a champion at arguing and Christina wanted to bark back: *Well, your father is ruining my life and the lives of my friends!* But Wink was shuffling around, trying to get comfortable, and the nine-year-old was darling but heavier than she looked, and Wink really should let her grandfather and Janice know she was okay. Her Inner Christina hissed, *Don't make things worse!*

"Of course," Christina said politely. "I'll do it right now."

She tucked her phone away. "Wink, let's go in the house. Everyone will be so glad to see you."

"Oh, Christina, can't I come stay with you? For just one night?"

Christina hugged Wink. "Maybe another night. Your grandfather is worried and it's getting late." She opened the door and twisted around and Wink pretzeled out onto the driveway. Christina took her hand and led her up to the door.

She knocked. Janice opened the door with a worried face.

"She's fine," Christina said. "She was hiding in the backseat of my car."

Janice exclaimed happily and bent down to fold the little girl in her arms. "Wink, we were so worried!"

"I'm cold," Wink said. "Could I have some hot chocolate?"

"Absolutely. With *two* marshmallows. Come in now and show your grandfather you're okay."

Little girls were like very short secret agents, much more cunning than expected with their sweet innocent faces, Christina thought. "Janice," she said, "we've called Delia and she's talked to Wink. I've got to get home now."

"Of course. Thanks, Christina."

Christina hugged Wink and said goodbye to Janice. Her car was waiting for her, still warm. She drove slowly down the hill and through the town.

The shops were busy and the sidewalks were crowded with people heading into restaurants and bars for some Christmas cheer. Couples wore Santa hats and long-tailed, striped elf hats. Some had dogs on leashes, and the dogs wore headbands of reindeer antlers. It was a cheerful scene, but Christina wasn't touched by it tonight. She had done her best, but she'd been unable to change Oscar's mind.

Back at home, she plugged in the lights of the Christmas tree and fed Mittens her canned "pâté" and changed out of her work clothes into her cozy robe. She had promised to call Andy to tell him how the meeting went, but she wanted to catch her emotional breath first. In November, she'd made several containers of lasagna and frozen them for these busy December nights. She popped one into the microwave and poured herself a glass of red wine. Curling up on the sofa, she enjoyed her easy meal while she watched a charming British mystery made from Ann Cleeves's books.

Christina knew that while she relaxed, the back of her mind was dashing around, all neurons and synapses quietly working on the Oscar problem.

When the program ended, she carried her plate and glass into the kitchen and washed up. Doing dishes calmed her somehow, it was like meditating while getting something accomplished. Never mind Oscar, she thought. She was ready to call Andy, but she had to be sensible and acknowledge to herself that while the electricity between them was powerful, she couldn't count on a long-term relationship.

Then, as if she and Andy were invisibly in sync, her phone buzzed, and it was him.

"Finally!" he announced. "I've finished my business meetings. Now tell me how your meeting went with Oscar."

"It didn't go well, I'm afraid. In fact, it turned into a dramatic three-ring circus." She told him about her conversation with Oscar, who would not give an inch on the rent raise, and how innocent Wink had blurted out that Oscar didn't need money, he needed friends. How Oscar had yelled at Wink, telling her to get out of his house, when Christina was certain the older man meant she should leave the room, and how Wink disappeared, and everyone was worried, and then Wink popped up in Christina's car, and finally the drama was over when Wink returned to her grandfather's house.

"So," Andy said jokingly, "not a successful meeting."

"No."

"I'm sorry, Christina. Delia and I are used to Oscar's temper. Hell, everyone who works with him knows he can blow at any moment. But I'm surprised and angry that he yelled at Wink."

"Wink is fine," Christina assured him. "We talked about it in the car. I told her that Oscar was mad at me, not her. She was smiling when I took her to the house, and Janice met her at the door and offered her hot chocolate." Christina paused. "Delia's not very happy with me."

"My family." Andy sighed. "We're really not as awful as we seem. Look, I'll be back on the island tomorrow. Let me take you somewhere fun, somewhere festive."

"I'd love that, Andy. Tomorrow night is the Nantucket Music Community Center's Holiday Chorus Concert. It's always gorgeous." Defensively, she added, "Many of the singers have sung in New York or Boston; some are professional but use Nantucket as a vacation home—"

"That sounds great, Christina. What time?"

"It's four in the afternoon, which means I'll close my shop early, but I wouldn't miss this for the world."

"After that, I'll take you out to dinner."

"Or, after that, we can go to Mimi's Christmas party, where you'll get more than enough to eat and drink."

"Great! Should I wear a tie?"

"If you have a Christmas-themed tie, yes, but I'd bet my bottom dollar you don't possess such a thing."

"You're right. I don't."

"Good to know. Now I know what to tell Wink to get you for Christmas."

"I look forward to that!"

They continued to talk, easily bantering, joking, or letting silence fall between them. Christina felt as if she'd known Andy for hundreds of years. She could almost believe in past lives.

As they talked about their childhood Christmases, Christina turned off all the lights except those on the Christmas tree. She stretched out on her sofa, covering her legs with a red, green, and white throw. In the corner, the tree glowed steadily, filling the air with gentle colors. This was perfection, her warm quiet house, the Christmas tree, and Andy's voice as close to her as if they lay on pillows in a bed.

12

The bright, mild day brought shoppers out in droves. Christina didn't want to close for lunch, but she had to talk to the other Shedders about what had transpired the night before, so she put up a sign that said BACK IN TEN MINUTES, locked her door, and raced over to Mimi's.

"I can't stay long," Christina said.

"Nor can we," Mimi told her. "Isn't it wonderful, all the business we're getting!"

"Hurry up and tell us what happened," Harriet said.

"Basically," Christina told them, "he said he wants his ten percent or he wants us gone."

"Did you tell him about the community?" Harriet asked.

"Of course I did. He doesn't care about the community. He cares about money. He said that, and little Wink was in the room with us. And she tried to argue with him and he told her to get out of the house."

"Oh, dear," Mimi said. "Poor little girl."

"Poor little girl, my aunt Mabel," Harriet snapped. "She'll grow up rich and be as haughty as the rest of them."

"Delia isn't haughty," Jacob said. "She's shy."

"Jacob Greenwood!" Mimi clapped her hands and laughed. "Do you have somethin' goin' on with Delia Lombard!"

"We're acquaintances. That's all. I met her at Christina's tree decorating party and we know some of the same people from school."

"I can't believe this!" Harriet exploded. "How come you two are hooking up with that family? It should be *me*." She was on the verge of tears.

"Harriet," Christina said. "It doesn't matter what we do with anyone in that family. We still have to agree to pay ten percent more for our sheds, and that is the cold hard truth."

"Maybe I could hook up with Oscar," Mimi said.

Everyone stared in horror.

"Just kidding," Mimi told them. "Just a little desperate attempt at humor." Sighing, she leaned against a counter stacked with merchandise. "Look, everyone, we might as well go back to work and be glad we're too busy to eat lunch. Christina did her best but she's right. We've got to decide what to do. But not now. Now we'll enjoy Christmas. And we'll have fun tonight at my party, right? Wear your ugliest Christmas sweater."

"As if I even have one," Harriet scoffed.

Christina stepped from her warm shower into a bathroom swirling with steam. She was determined to enjoy Christmas tonight. She wouldn't allow herself to worry about the hike in rent.

Last year at the January sale at Vis-A-Vis, she'd bought a sensational red silk dress and tonight was the perfect time to wear it. She could wear her highest heels, because no snow or ice had yet turned the sidewalks and streets into hazard zones.

She tied her long brown hair back with a green Christmas ribbon. She frosted her lips with her most shimmering red lip gloss. She looked *good*.

"Wow!" Andy said when he came to the door. "I don't know whether to put you on a pedestal or ravage you."

Christina laughed. "Just don't smear my lip gloss."

"Oh, you can always redo your lip gloss," Andy teased, and took Christina in his arms and kissed her firmly.

Christina's legs went weak and her heart did flips. She pulled away. "We have to go. We don't want to be late for the concert."

In the car on the way to the performance, they chatted idly about their days. Neither of them mentioned her unpleasant meeting with Oscar. The church was packed and decked out with Christmas wreaths, and entering the nave lifted her heart. She knew everyone in the chorus, or almost everyone, and that added a special pleasure to the event. It was good, Christina thought, that she and Andy would spend most of this evening with other people. That way they would have no time for a serious talk.

And really, she didn't know what she wanted to say.

Could she tell Andy that she was breaking it off with him because his father was such a miser? She had strong, honest feelings for Andy, but could she possibly think that they could be together long-term when his father was a mean, unpleasant, cranky old scrooge with a heart of ice?

The music was heavenly. Her thoughts were not.

After the concert, they drove to Mimi's party.

"I bet you can tell which house is Mimi's," Christina said as they turned onto Mimi's street.

"Could it possibly be the one with the sleigh and reindeer on the roof, Frosty on one side of the yard, and the crèche and wise men and even a donkey on the other side?"

Christina laughed. "Mimi really likes Christmas. Since her husband, Jude, died, the neighbors help put up this light show every year."

They had to park down the block because so many cars were already there. Inside the house, laurel wrapped the staircase handrail, elves hung from picture frames, and angels swung from the chandelier over the dining room table. Anything that couldn't move was tied with red and green ribbon.

The house was packed with people, so Christina took Andy's hand to lead him to the bedroom where they dropped their coats. The dining room table was laden with cheeses, a ham, biscuits and honey, crackers and dip, and about a hundred different kinds of Christmas cookies.

"Come with me," Christina yelled at Andy. "I want you to meet Mimi."

They found her in the kitchen, slicing a three-layer Christmas cake.

"So nice to meet you!" Mimi said over her shoulder. "Go drink some eggnog. You'll like me much better after you've had a cup."

Christina laughed and guided Andy back into the noisy mass of the party. They found the creamy, frothy eggnog in a crystal bowl in the living room and ladled themselves each a cup.

Andy coughed after his first sip. "What's in this?"

Christina said, "I think the main ingredients are ice cream and brandy."

"Hey," Andy said. "There's my sister. I didn't know she was coming."

Christina turned. Delia wore a green velvet dress. Her hair was in an upsweep. She looked very pretty, and Jacob seemed to think so, too, as he leaned close to hear her.

"*Who* is Jacob?" Andy asked Christina.

"That's what I want to know!" Harriet, wearing an extremely low-cut gold dress, accosted Christina, clutching her arm, maybe to get Christina's attention, but maybe to help herself get her balance.

"I mean really," Harriet continued. "You're her brother, tell me why she's stalking Jacob."

"I don't believe she's stalking—"

Harriet interrupted. "Okay, fine. But look at them! I'm prettier than she is."

Christina intervened, pushing Harriet to the left to help her stand straight. "Harriet, this is my friend Andy. Andy, I believe Harriet has had a little too much eggnog."

"And that's all I'll have," Harriet lamented. "You and Jacob will swan off with the rich kids and I'll just drink eggnog and get fat."

Before Christina could decide what to say, Danny Folger appeared with a plate full of food. After a quick nod to

Christina and Andy, he said to Harriet, "I got you some goodies. Come sit with me and let's eat."

Danny Folger was one of the island's favorite sons. He was without a doubt one of the most handsome men on Nantucket, with his construction worker's muscles and his thick blond hair. He'd been trying to date Harriet for months, but even though his family was one of the first families of the island, he wasn't rich and he certainly wasn't cultured. He'd rather rake for scallops than sit through a symphony, and he'd never make enough money to give Harriet the mansion she dreamed of.

Poor Danny, Christina thought, but thank heavens he was taking care of Harriet. Christina didn't want to be the one to see that Harriet got safely home on this cold night.

Christina and Andy set their eggnog aside and returned to the table where plates and utensils were stacked. They filled their plates and wandered through the party. Christina introduced Andy to some of her friends, and at one point they found themselves with Delia and Jacob.

"I want to apologize for the other night," Delia said. "I'm sorry I was so rude about Wink. I was afraid she'd run away and, frankly, I wouldn't blame her. This divorce is hard on her and Oscar has been her hero. I'm sure it shocked her terribly when he told her to leave the room."

"He told her to leave the *house*," Christina corrected.

"That's not what he says he said."

"But I was there. I heard him. Don't you think Wink's reaction was so strong because he said *house*?"

In response, Delia turned to Andy with a sad face. "Do you think Father is losing it?"

"No," Andy said. "It's normal for people his age to mix up their words, especially under emotional stress. Dad needs to slow down. He works too hard."

Delia laughed. "You can tell him that." She turned back to Christina. "I apologize again for bringing our family problems into your pleasant evening. I think I should leave now. I told Wink she could stay up until I came home to put her to bed. She and I have a busy day tomorrow, so she won't be able to help you."

"That's fine," Christina said. "Give her my love."

Jacob moved closer to Delia. "I'll drive you home now if you like."

"I'd like," Delia replied, and she sounded absolutely sultry.

"What's going on there?" Christina asked Andy as Jacob escorted Delia from the room.

Andy shrugged. "Do you think she tells me anything? I'm just glad she's having a good time with someone. This divorce business is hard on her. I think she's overwhelmed."

They circled the food table again, choosing cookies and sweets. Friends of Christina's wandered up to say hello. Christina introduced them to Andy. After a while, she didn't mention his surname, but merely said, "This is my friend Andy," because the name Bittlesman was so impressive people forgot to talk and simply stared. But some of her friends already knew who he was and were glad to see him. Peter Berry talked to him about deep-sea fishing and promised to take him out some summer day. Bart Manville invited Andy to ride out to Great Point to see the seals. And two of Christina's prettiest friends who ran shops in town invited Andy to stop by their stores. They were full of Christmas cheer and winked at Christina as they chatted with Andy. Christina rolled her eyes at them.

It was nearly eleven when the crowd began to thin out.

"I should go home," Christina told Andy. "Busy day tomorrow."

Back in the car, Andy said, "I like your friends. Especially Peter and Bart. You know a lot of cool people."

Christina smiled. "I do. Nantucket attracts cool people. Or you could call them eccentrics. A lot of environmentalists live here—well, you and your father are aware of that. The world is changing, and this island, because it's an isolated area, is a good place to test stuff like ocean water quality, eel grass, bird migration, and climate change."

"You feel like you belong here," Andy said.

"I do. I wouldn't want to live anywhere else."

Andy was quiet after that.

When he pulled into her driveway, Christina asked him in for a drink.

He put the car in park but left it running. "I'd like to come in, but I don't know if I should." Andy paused. "Oh, man, I really want to kiss you."

Christina leaned forward.

They sat in the car kissing like a pair of teenagers until Andy's elbow hit the horn. They jumped apart.

"I hope I didn't wake people up," Andy said.

Christina smiled. "I don't care if you did. But I've got to go inside. Really. Until Christmas Day, my business takes priority."

"Before you go, Christina . . . this is awkward. I wish I

could help you with my father and the rent hike. But I'm afraid Father would be resistant to anything I propose. He and I are locked in a battle right now. He wants me to stay in New York. I want to move here. This is a tough time for him, too, with Delia getting divorced. He's getting old and losing control. I want to get through Christmas before going to war with him."

"I understand, Andy. Christmas is always such an intense time. So emotional."

"I'll be here after Christmas," Andy said. "I'd like to be with you, Christina. I'd like to be with you all the time."

Christina raised her hand to her forehead. What was Andy saying? It was too enormous to take in. "Can we wait just a few days to talk about the future? I've got to concentrate on this rent problem before I can focus on anything else. I need to get some rest for tomorrow."

Andy nodded. "I understand. Let me walk you to your door."

"Fine," Christina said, "but no more kissing. I'm sure some neighbors woke up to that horn blast and are peering out their curtains to see what I'm up to."

Andy grinned. "We could give them something to talk about."

She punched his arm lightly.

He walked her to the door, gave her a gentle peck on the lips, and returned to his car.

Christina entered her house. Before taking off her coat, she plugged in the Christmas tree lights.

"Mittens," she said to the cat yawning on the sofa, "I believe I have stars in my eyes."

13

Christina awoke with a smile on her face. Mittens slept in her usual place in the curl of Christina's knees. The cat purred loudly, content to be lazy and warm. Outside her window, the sky was a clear bright blue—it would be a perfect shopping day. She was eager to get to work, but for just a few more minutes she allowed herself to snuggle into her warm pillows and remember last night.

Especially the part of last night when she and Andy were kissing.

And the way he'd looked at her when he walked her to her door. She knew she saw love in his eyes, she'd felt it all the way into her heart. They had something special between them, she was sure of it, and everything else, including her shop, was somehow swept up in the magic glow of love. It would all work out. It would all be fine.

She rose, pulled on her L.L.Bean flannel robe, slid her feet into her warm fleece-lined slippers, and went down to the kitchen. She started her coffee maker, then opened the back door. The day was magnificent! Clear and crisp—and cold, yes, but the kind of cold that brightened her spirits.

"Deck the halls with boughs of holly!" Christina sang. Suddenly she was overflowing with song and a sense of good will and celebration. Shivering, she closed the door, turned back to the kitchen, and quickly opened a can of food for Mittens, who clearly did not feel uplifted by her singing. Christina ate a piece of toast thick with butter and cherry preserves and drank a cup of coffee while she made her lunch. Taking another cup of coffee with her, she went upstairs and showered, still singing. By the time she'd finished all the verses of "The Twelve Days of Christmas," she was out of the shower and ready to dress, and she was in such a good mood—such a *Christmasy* mood—that she paired her best sweater, a green cashmere pullover, with yoga pants and knee-high red boots. She chose her brightest red lipstick and added her Christmas bell earrings. Standing in front of her mirror, she assessed herself. She looked gorgeous and festive. Maybe a bit over the top, too, but if she couldn't do it this close to Christmas, when could she?

It was too cold to bike to work, so she drove to Union Street and parked in a summer friend's driveway. She strode toward the wharf in her A-line red wool coat, and the hem flipped with each step. She waved at passing acquaintances, and then as she stepped onto the brick wharf, she slowed down and paid attention to each step. Bricks were beautiful and historic, but easy to slip on, even in the summer.

"Merry Christmas!" she called to Mimi, who was just opening her shop.

"Merry Christmas!" Mimi called back.

She passed Jacob's shed and Harriet's, and saw the lights of their shops spring to life. To her delight, she had customers waiting by her own door.

"Merry Christmas!" she greeted them. "Come in!"

The hours sped by as she knew they would, with people of all ages rushing in and out. Wooden baby rattles, child-size picnic baskets, mermaids, pirates, ships, and lighthouses were snatched up triumphantly. "The perfect present!" several people cried.

Christina was so pleased to see their joy at finding just the right thing. She couldn't believe it when the town clock struck noon. The store emptied out as people rushed off to meet friends and family for lunch.

Her phone buzzed. Delia had texted: *I'm going to have Wink with me all day. We're going to do some Christmas shopping. Actually, she probably won't be able to "work" with you anymore. Thank you for giving her something fun to do.*

"*Well,* damn!" her Inner Christina said.

"It's all right," Christina said aloud as she stood alone in her shop. "I was only being nice to a little girl."

Yeah, too bad that little girl stole your heart, her IC said.

"I'll see Wink again," Christina said bravely. "It's only right that she's with her mother."

She looked around her darling shop. It was rather chaotic. She needed to organize the toys. But for a moment, she allowed herself to admit that she missed Wink. Maybe someday she'd have a daughter of her own . . .

She was getting moody. She considered texting Andy or even calling him just to hear his voice, but she knew she needed to sit down, eat lunch, and drink some coffee if she was going to make it through the rest of the day. So she picked up her handsome briefcase, which held only her wallet, her phone, a bottle of water, and a humble peanut butter and jelly sandwich. She stepped outside, locked her door, and looked up at the sky. Not a cloud. Too bad. It was cold enough to snow. It must be way below freezing, she thought. She'd ask Jacob. He'd know.

She set off down the wharf toward Mimi's shed, feeling quite fabulous in her red coat and knee-high red leather boots. She wished Andy could see her now!

And there, about thirty steps away, was Andy! He wore his black wool coat with a red and white striped muffler around his throat. He waved at her with gloved hands.

"Andy!" she called, waving back, and only then did she notice the woman next to him.

She was a very noticeable woman, over six feet tall in her knee-high black patent leather boots, a black suede coat with fur trim at the cuffs and hem, and an enormous Cossack fur hat. Her green eyes glittered over swooping cheekbones, and her mouth was a plump bow.

Anastasiya Belousova.

Andy's ex-girlfriend. Obviously not so ex.

Christina's heart sank right to her toes. She forced herself to keep smiling, she wouldn't let herself seem hurt that Anastasiya was there, but—

With a crack and a roar, the world exploded. In an instant, the bricks beneath Christina's feet split apart as a powerful geyser blasted upward, drenching her with icy water and knocking her to the ground.

"AAAAH!" she screamed as her back hit the bricks and her feet flew into the air, shoved upward by the powerful fountain.

"Look, Mommy, that lady fell down," a little boy said. "Maybe a whale is spouting under her."

"Don't go near her, Georgie, you might get wet."

"But I want to see!"

"Hold my hand and we'll stand over here."

"It's a broken water main," a man yelled. "Call the DPW!"

Harriet popped out of her shop. "Christina!" she called. "Are you all right?"

Christina didn't have the breath to answer. She was struggling to sit up, or to roll over and stand, but the strength of the geyser forced her down. Her body was shivering with cold, and her mind was overwhelmed, trying to understand what had just happened, and what she could do. She felt like an overturned beetle caught in a storm. She knew she looked like that, too, as she waved her arms and legs.

"Call the fire department," a woman said.

"Call 911," a man repeated.

"Christina!" Andy yelled as he raced down the wharf toward her, rushed into the rocketing torrent, gripped Christina under her arms, and hoisted her out and away from the streaming broken bricks.

By now a crowd had gathered. A siren sounded, coming closer. People stared, and some cheered when Andy pulled Christina away into the cold dry air, but it was all surreal to Christina. She shook so hard her teeth rattled.

Mimi rushed out of her shop. "Dear Lord, Christina,

are you okay? Andy, bring her inside, we can warm her up until an ambulance gets here."

As if she weighed less than a butterfly, Andy scooped Christina up in a bridal carry, as if they had just been married, and carefully made his way over the stones, which were now covered with ice, to Mimi's.

Just as they reached Mimi's door, a husky, exotic voice said, "She has no hat. She needs a hat to keep her head warm. Most important."

And just like that, Anastasiya Belousova plucked her huge silk-lined fur Cossack hat off her head and settled it onto Christina's.

"Thank you," Christina said through her chattering teeth. The warmth of the hat was miraculous. "I'm fine, Andy, put me down," she said, struggling to escape his arms.

He didn't let her go until Mimi pointed out a certain chair. He carefully deposited Christina on the chair, and Mimi bustled around moving all the space heaters close to Christina.

Christina was crying. She didn't know when she'd started crying, but she was aware that she wasn't crying in a particularly dignified or attractive way. She covered her face with her hands and her sobs came out like honks. Her mascara was running down her face, she could feel it, or maybe it was just leftover water. She didn't want Andy and his model girlfriend seeing her like this, although she knew they'd seen her humiliating pratfall, and her face must have been clown-like at the surprise of the sturdy, reliable floor of her world shattering beneath her.

Harriet came into Christina's range of vision. Taking Christina's hands, she tugged off Christina's gloves and, with difficulty, pulled her own dry gloves onto Christina's hands.

"Th-th-thank you," Christina stammered.

"Broken water pipe," Harriet said. "You should sue the town. You could get thousands."

"Darling, you are wet, also," said a deep, husky voice.

Christina glanced over to see Andy. His hair and face were dripping water. The arms and the front of his coat were drenched. Her heart surged with joy to know how he had raced down the wharf toward her and dived into the downpour to pull her out. Could anything be more story-book romantic?

Then she heard Anastasiya say, "Bend down."

Through her tears, Christina watched Andy tilt his head forward. Anastasiya had found a roll of paper towels. With the easy authority of one who knew his body well, Anastasiya dried Andy's hair, laughing at how it stood up in all directions. She patted his face and neck dry and blotted water off the shoulders and front of his coat. Through it all, she murmured to Andy in Russian, her husky voice rich with affection.

Christina tried to pull herself together.

"Let us through, please," a man said, and Christina was aware of two people in high-vis jackets coming toward her with a stretcher.

"A stretcher!" she protested. "Don't carry me out on a stretcher!" Could she possibly be even more humiliated in front of Andy and Anastasiya?

"Christina, you're in shock," Mimi told her.

The EMTs ignored her, quickly lifting her up and setting her down on the stretcher, instantly covering her with a foil Mylar blanket.

"We'll follow you to the hospital," Andy said.

We, Christina thought. "No!" she yelled. "Please don't come!"

Then she was slid into the ambulance, an EMT sat beside her, and the heavy doors were slammed shut.

The ambulance bumped over the bricks toward the hospital, siren wailing. The EMTs put a blood pressure cuff on one arm and an IV in the other.

"W-w-what's that?" Christina sobbed.

"Only a saline solution with some electrolytes to stabilize you," Misty LaRosa answered. Misty was only a few years older than Christina; in spite of her gentle name, she had the personality of a lacrosse coach.

"Misty, this isn't necessary," Christina said. "I'm fine, just wet. I just need to go home."

"You're in shock, your temperature has dropped, and this is hospital policy."

Christina knew better than to argue with hospital policy.

It was only a five-minute drive to the hospital. As they sped along, the male EMT pulled off Christina's poor ruined red boots and soggy socks and wrapped Christina's feet and legs in a warm blanket. The feeling was heavenly. With a screech, the ambulance turned, and before she could think twice, the doors were open and she was being lifted onto a rolling hospital bed and rushed into an emergency room. A privacy curtain was pulled around her. Someone removed the IV.

"Open your mouth," someone said, and quickly inserted a thermometer.

"Can you sit up, sweetheart?" a female nurse asked.

Christina recognized Annette O'Brien, another island woman a few years older than she was, a goodhearted, cheerful acquaintance.

Christina nodded and sat up, swinging her legs over the side of the bed. Somehow her feet had been encased in warm hospital booties.

"What the dickens happened?" Annette asked.

"I guess the water pipe broke," Christina said. "It leads out to the restrooms and restaurant at the end of the wharf and I was walking there . . ." Because she knew Annette, because she knew Annette was a good, sympathetic woman, Christina let herself go. "Oh, Annette, I was so frightened! I didn't know what happened. It was like a monster had smashed up from the water through the wharf, or maybe the end of the world, or a bomb, I couldn't understand, it all happened so fast."

Annette put her arms around Christina and hugged her. "Poor girl," she said, patting Christina's back. "How scary. But you're all right. You've had a shock, sweetheart, but you'll be just fine." Stepping away, she said, "You fell on your back, right? Can you stand up so we can get your wet clothes off and put you in a warm robe?"

Holding on to Annette's arms, Christina slid down to the floor. When she tried to pull the sleeve of her cashmere sweater off, it stuck to her skin.

"Here, dear, let me do it. You just relax." Annette chattered away as she undressed Christina. "Nice cashmere sweater, and you know the good thing about wool is it stays warm even when it's wet. Okay, now put your arms out, I'm slipping a johnny on you. Turn around, I'll tie it in the back. And bless my soul! You landed right on your tailbone, my dear. You've got a lovely little bump there. We'll lie you on your side and I'll put an ice pack next to it."

"Oh, not an *ice* pack!" Christina begged.

Annette laughed. "All right, my darling, no ice pack until you are nice and cozy warm. Now hold out your arms, I'm putting a robe on you, and then we'll get you back in bed and under the covers and tucked up snug."

Christina held out her arms. She felt like a child with her mother dressing her, and it was a comforting sensation.

"Now what shall we do about your lovely fur hat?" Annette asked.

"It's not *my* hat!" Christina cried.

"If you say so, Christina, but it's on your head. Shall we take it off? I know it's giving you warmth, but I'd bet your hair is wet under there. We need to wrap your hair in towels."

Christina lifted her arms and removed the Cossack hat—the dark fur was silky in her hands. "Do you think it's mink?" she asked Annette.

Annette examined the hat, turning it this way and that. "No, it's not mink, it's faux fur. It says so on the label right here."

Christina had almost stopped weeping but at this news

she burst into helpless sobs. "Not only is she beautiful, she's an animal lover!"

"Well, let's worry about all that later. Let's get you in bed for now."

"I'm really fine," Christina said. "I need to get back to my shop."

"Yes, and I'm sure you'll be able to once the doctor checks you over," Annette said. She helped Christina onto the bed and covered her in soft blankets. "Just close your eyes and rest a wee bit now. I'll be back."

Christina obeyed. Warmth melted into her body, her muscles relaxed, and her breathing slowed.

Annette returned to the room. "Christina, there's a young man insisting on seeing you. His name is Andy Bittlesman."

Christina snorted. "Give that young man his girlfriend's fur hat and tell him to go away."

"Whatever you say."

Annette left. A few moments later she was back. "He says to tell you she's not his girlfriend."

"She dried him off!" Christina blurted, and her tears started up again.

Annette looked puzzled. "If you don't want to see him, you don't have to."

With her bright blue down coat rustling, Mimi rushed into the room.

"They said I could come in," Mimi told her. "I've got your briefcase. When you fell, it slid away from you, so it didn't get wet."

"Good." Christina sat up, holding a blanket around her

shoulders. "My cell and wallet are in there. Thanks, Mimi. But what are you doing here? What about your shop?"

"The DPW has closed off that section of the wharf while they fix the broken pipe," Mimi told her. "They've sanded the area where the water froze and it's off-limits."

"You're losing business!" Christina cried. "I'm so sorry!"

Mimi plopped down on the bed next to Christina and hugged her close. "Don't worry about that. We'll be fine. Once word gets around town about the pipe breaking, people will swarm to check it out and they'll stop by our shops. It's great publicity. The most important thing is, how are you?"

Warmed by Mimi's affection, Christina said, "Physically? I'm fine, except for a bump on my bum. Emotionally, I'm a basket case."

"Of course you are," Mimi said, hugging Christina tighter. "That must have been a terrifying few moments."

"It was. But something else . . . just before the pipe burst, I saw Andy walking with his girlfriend."

"Oh, crackers!" Mimi exclaimed. "I saw her, too. Anastasiya Belousova. They say she's the most beautiful woman on this planet. Her eyes are amazing, like a husky dog's eyes. I mean, really, Anastasiya Belousova on our little island!"

Christina turned her head away to hide her tears.

"Oh, dear. I'm sorry, Christina. I'm such a dunce. I forgot you're seeing Andy."

"I'm afraid that's past tense," Christina said bitterly.

"Oh, sweetie, not necessarily."

"Then why were they walking down the wharf together?

Why is she even on the island? Andy told me they'd broken up." She snorted. "And I believed him." Then, in spite of herself, she asked, "Is Andy still out in the hall? With Anastasiya?"

"I didn't see him."

Christina slowly shook her head. "So he left. They left."

"You mean they were here before I got here?"

"Yes."

"Did Andy come talk with you?"

"I told the nurse to give him his girlfriend's fur hat and to tell him to go away."

"Yes, I saw Anastasiya put it on your head. That was nice of her, don't you think?"

"Oh, of course," Christina said crabbily. "She's a real live angel."

Mimi sighed. "You're overreacting. You don't know the facts. You don't know why she's here, and if Andy left the hospital, it's what you told him to do. Listen, sweetheart, Jacob's going to buzz me when I can open my shop again, so I'll have to rush off." As she spoke, Mimi's phone buzzed. She held it up to Christina, waved, and stepped out of the room.

"Thanks for coming, Mimi," Christina called.

The privacy curtain rattled as a white-coated physician entered the room. It was Dr. Fegley, a brusque but beloved older man who'd seen generations of Nantucketers grow up.

"Hello, Christina. I hear you've had a little adventure."

"Not such an adventure," Christina said. The doctor's presence made her sniff back her tears and sit up straight.

He'd been her doctor since she was a child. "A water main broke. I fell. I bumped my bum and got cold, but basically, I'm okay."

"Let's just check you out." Dr. Fegley went through the usual routine. "Do you hurt anywhere?" he said.

Christina sniffed. "My pride's hurt, that's all. It was really humiliating."

"You're young. I'm not worried about your pride." Dr. Fegley stepped back. "Actually, I'm not worried about you at all. Your temperature is normal, you're showing no signs of disorientation or dizziness or nausea. Anything you want to mention? Headache? Double vision?"

"Nothing like that. I'm hungry, that's all. I missed my lunch."

The physician laughed and patted her knee. "I'd say you're good to go. You can always call me if you start to feel faint."

"I will. Thanks, Dr. Fegley."

He left her little private space. For a few moments, Christina sat on the hospital bed, her legs dangling, trying to gather her thoughts. She'd never considered herself a dependent sort of person, the kind of person people had to help. In one moment, that changed. It would take a while for her to recover—not physically, but emotionally, from that bizarre, incomprehensible moment when the ground exploded under her feet.

She didn't know if she'd ever recover from the humiliating fact that Andy and his perfect girlfriend had seen her flailing around with her legs in the air like an overturned beetle, grasping for something to hold on to, spitting water out of her mouth as fast as it hit her in the face. Not a pretty sight.

But more important than her fall was the reality that Andy had been right there, walking with his girlfriend. True, while other people stood gawking, Andy had rushed into the torrent and pulled Christina free. He had lifted and carried her like a hero on the front of a romance novel. And he'd come to the hospital to see how she was. But that was something any friend would do, she supposed. And, indeed, the beautiful Anastasiya came with him—if Andy really cared for Christina, would he bring his ex-girlfriend with him? Of course not.

Which meant that Anastasiya was no longer an ex. Which meant Andy was coming to tell Christina that he was back together with the gorgeous model.

You don't know *that,* her Inner Christina pointed out. *Stop trying to make things worse than they are.*

"I'm bruised. I fell on my ass in front of Andy and his exotic model lover! All my clothes are wet, and I'm all alone!" Christina retorted, and she was so emotional she didn't care that she'd said it all out loud. After all, she was talking to her imaginary inner self.

"Maybe I'm crazy, too," she whispered, and buried her face in her hands, letting the tears fall.

14

"They said you were in here."

To Christina's surprise, Harriet came through the curtain. She wore a clever green beret over her long blond hair—only Harriet could carry off a beret—that accentuated her green eyes. She had a hatbox with the words NANTUCKET COUTURE printed on the side.

"I've brought you some clothes," she said.

"Oh, thank you, Harriet." Harriet being nice? How many more shocks could Christina take? She quickly wiped the tears from her face and forced a smile.

Harriet set the hatbox on the bed and opened it. "I know what you're thinking. I'm not a complete monster. That must have been so frightening. And you looked so ridiculous, wriggling around on your back like an over-turned turtle. Thank heavens it didn't happen to me."

Christina burst out laughing. "Always Harriet, all the time!"

"I'm only saying what everyone else thinks. And I'm here, aren't I? Mimi had to go back to her store. The wharf is open now. It's above freezing, so there's no ice and it's safe to walk there. I know you want to get back to your shop so I raced home to get you something to wear."

"That's so thoughtful, Harriet. I hadn't even considered how I would dress to leave."

"Well, here. You can wear this while I drive you to your house for your own clothes. Try this tunic with the tights. It might work."

Christina slid off the bed, peeled off the hospital robe and johnny and slipped the tunic over her head. It fit, but oddly. Harriet had a voluptuous figure, and Christina was more slender and small-boned. The dress sagged around the bosom and hips. When she pulled on the tights, they drooped and crinkled. The two women grinned at each other.

"I don't have any shoes," Christina said. She pointed to her soggy red boots that someone had deposited beneath a chair. "Those were so expensive and they're ruined."

"Nonsense," Harriet said briskly. "Stuff them with newspaper and let them dry. They'll be fine."

"I'll try." At the moment, Christina had little hope for anything being fine. She looked down at her feet wrapped in the hospital's paper slippers. "I can't walk in these."

"I'll pull the car right up to the door and then I'll drive you home. You can tolerate it that far. Then I'll drive you in to work."

Christina teared up again. Her emotions were all over the place. "You're so nice, Harriet."

Harriet snorted. "You're just in shock. Here, I brought you one of my coats." With a few brisk movements, Harriet put Christina's sodden clothes into a large clear trash bag. "Okay? Good to go?"

"My hair . . ." Christina pushed it away from her face. "It must look like a bird's nest."

"I've seen it look worse," Harriet said with a wicked grin. "Let's go."

The new hospital was enormous, and for a few minutes, they had to concentrate on finding their way out. Finally they arrived at the front desk. Harriet went off to get her car while Christina checked out, and suddenly Christina was sitting in Harriet's slightly beaten-up MG convertible. It was Harriet's pride and joy, and a sign to everyone that she was classy, but it was so low to the ground Christina thought they might drive right under some of the trucks in front of them.

Harriet waited in the living room while Christina pulled her long brown hair back into a ponytail. She tugged on warm black Lululemons, an oversize blue cashmere sweater, and tossed on a white scarf covered with blue penguins—last year's Christmas gift from Mimi. Thankful that she was a bit of a shoe addict, she slipped her feet into a pair of high black boots.

She hurried down the stairs. "Thanks for waiting, Harriet. I'm ready."

Harriet scrutinized Christina. "You don't look very Christmasy."

"I don't care. I'm warm."

"Well, your hair looks nice. I suppose that's one good thing about having curly hair."

Christina laughed. Would Harriet ever be able to give a

compliment without adding some kind of reservation? Oh, it didn't matter. Harriet had taken the time to fetch her from the hospital and that meant a lot.

Harriet found a parking space in front of Jewel in the Sea, so the two women didn't have far to walk to their shops. They headed down lower Main toward the wharf. The sky was blue and the air was almost balmy.

"Isn't it ever going to snow?" Christina complained. "It's Christmas, for heaven's sake!"

"I don't believe it," Harriet said.

"What?" Christina turned to see Harriet a few steps behind her, in front of the restaurant b-ACK yard BBQ.

Christina went to stand next to Harriet. Through the large plate glass window, she saw Delia Bittlesman having lunch with Jacob. They were engrossed with each other, leaning forward so far their heads almost touched.

"Bastard," Harriet said.

Christina linked her arm through Harriet's. "Come on now, we can't stand here gaping at them." She dragged Harriet away from the restaurant window.

Harriet trudged along next to Christina, emitting an aura of misery. "Well, you saw him, too. Jacob's getting up close and personal with Delia." Harriet kicked at a pebble. "I wish those Bittlesmans had never come to the island."

"I agree," Christina said. "But listen, Harriet. I don't think your snotty persona is working with Jacob. I wish you'd try being nicer to everyone and *really* nice to him. You're beautiful. I think he'd respond well if you were . . . *softer* . . . with him."

Harriet sighed. "I'd just make a fool of myself."

"It takes courage to love someone," Christina said.

"Now you sound like a greeting card."

"Okay, that's enough from me. Come on, the wharf is swarming with shoppers."

Harriet pointed at a small square of land surrounded by sawhorses and yellow police tape. "The DPW certainly worked fast."

Christina's stomach dropped when she saw the site. She took Harriet's hands in hers. "Harriet, thank you for taking the time to help me. I'll treat you to dinner some night."

"You don't have to do that, Christina," Harriet said. "We're friends!"

"And we've got a lot to talk about!" Impulsively, Christina leaned over and kissed Harriet's cheek.

The women exchanged warm smiles and went their separate ways to open their shops. So something good had come out of this terrible day, Christina thought.

It felt wonderful to unlock the door and step inside her shop. It was cold, but that would change once she flicked on her little electric radiator. The room was familiar and orderly. Each shelf displayed wooden lighthouses, wicker picnic baskets, bejeweled mermaid books, all unpacked by her own hands and placed exactly where she wanted them. The small shop was bright and cheerful with color, all her treasures waiting expectantly to be discovered and cherished.

She loved this shop.

She was not going to let it be taken away by Oscar Bittlesman without a fight.

Christina was barely behind the counter with her coat off when customers flocked in. The rest of the afternoon she had no time to think, or to check her phone, which lay on a shelf beneath the cash register with her purse, pinging every five minutes, or so it seemed. When six o'clock arrived, darkness had fallen and a breeze had kicked up. By then, Christina was feeling the effects of her fall. She wanted to go home, curl up in front of the television, and drink chicken noodle soup. She turned off her electric radiator, locked her door, and carefully and quickly made her way over to her car on Union Street. She was glad she'd driven to work this morning. She didn't have the energy to bike home.

And it wasn't simply her body that ached. Her heart hurt so much when she thought of Andy that she whimpered. She was proud of herself for keeping it together all afternoon. She drove home, jacked up the heat, and turned on the Christmas tree lights. Mittens rubbed up against her ankles, mewing. The world might be coming to an end for Christina, but Mittens wanted her dinner, *now*.

Christina opened a can of Fancy Feast, set it in a clean bowl—Mittens liked her bowls clean—and put it on the floor for the cat. She was pouring herself a glass of wine when her phone buzzed. *Wink!*

"Christina, are you okay? Mommy said that Uncle Andy said that you had an accident!"

Christina was so touched by Wink's concern that she felt like *she* was nine years old. Maybe the Bittlesmans weren't such monsters after all, if Andy had thought to tell Delia and Delia had allowed Wink to call Christina.

"Christina? Are you there?"

Christina laughed. "I'm here, Wink, and I'm just fine. It was such a crazy thing! A water pipe broke beneath the bricks on the wharf and exploded right under me! For a moment I felt like I was on a ride at Disney World!"

"That's cool!" Wink laughed. "I wish I'd seen it!"

"I wish you'd seen it, too," Christina said.

"Mommy says we can come bring you dinner. Maybe soup."

Christina was so surprised she couldn't speak for a minute. "Sweetie, that's so nice of your mother, but it's not necessary. I wasn't hurt. I'm fine. I'm just about to step into a long, hot bath."

"Okay! Catch you later, alligator."

"After a while, crocodile."

She nibbled some cheese and crackers while she sipped her wine. Her phone buzzed again. *Andy.*

No. She couldn't deal with him tonight. She wasn't thinking clearly and she didn't want to say anything foolish because she was so emotional. She left the phone on the kitchen counter and went upstairs to take a hot bath. But the idea of water, even hot, was suddenly unappealing. She pulled on her warmest pajamas and crawled into bed. In a moment, she was asleep.

15

She opened her eyes to a new day. She fed Mittens, made coffee, and sat down to check her cellphone. It was dead. Of course it was, she hadn't charged it at all yesterday or last night. She plugged it in and took a shower and shampooed and blow-dried her hair and put on fresh clothes while the phone was charging.

Back in the kitchen, she tossed blueberries on her granola and sat down to eat while she scrolled through the messages on her phone. Her good friend Louise had called several times. Mimi and Harriet had called several times.

Andy had phoned about fifty times. He'd also left several voicemail messages.

The first few were versions of "Christina, I hope you're all right. I really want to speak with you."

The next one was longer. "Christina, I'm afraid you got the wrong idea. I want to explain about Anastasiya. She wasn't *with* me. We ran into each other on Main Street. She's engaged to Wonk, who's the running back for the Patriots. They're visiting Belichick, staying at one of his guesthouses on his compound. She was headed for the Hy-Line to make reservations because the forecast is for strong winds so planes can't fly. I was coming to see you, and we ran into each other. We had barely said hello when we saw you and then the pipe burst. Christina, you're the one I care about. Please believe me."

After that message, Christina shut off her phone.

Absentmindedly setting her cereal bowl on the floor so her cat could drink the milk, she leaned her chin in her hands and said, "Mittens, we have a lot to think about. I suppose what Andy said could be true. Okay, let's just walk out on a ledge and believe that what he said is true. I mean, if he was back with Anastasiya, why would he tell me those things?"

She turned on her phone. When it was ready, she scrolled through her contacts to find Andy's number.

She stopped, her finger trembling over his number.

"No, Mittens," she told the cat. "I've got to have it out with Oscar before I can be clear about Andy."

Mittens yawned.

Christina stood up. "I have an idea," she told Mittens. "A really good idea. I'm going to go see Oscar. I'm going to *challenge* the man."

Once again she dressed in her power outfit, the pantsuit and gold charm and Hermès scarf. She rolled her hair up into a messy bun like Meghan Markle's, and took time carefully and skillfully applying eyeliner and red lipstick. She carried her briefcase with her, even though only her wallet and a sandwich were in it. She had to wear her lumpy down coat because her wool coat had to go to the cleaners before she could wear it again. She pulled on a pair of red mittens, added a red wool cloche hat, and went out to her car.

She shook with nerves as she drove around the streets and up the brick road to the house on the cliff. She checked her lipstick in the visor mirror, picked up her briefcase, and strode to the door.

She knocked firmly on the door of Oscar Bittlesman's house.

"Christina!" Janice's eyes went wide with surprise. "What are you doing here? Everyone else has left—"

"Is Oscar here? He's the one I want to see."

"Well, yes, he's here, he's finishing his breakfast . . ."

Christina stepped over the threshold, making Janice back up in the process. Christina had a moment of guilty exhilaration. She felt kind of like a gangster.

"I won't take more than a moment," she told Janice.

"He's on the sunporch. Down the hall and to the right."

Christina strode down the hall, her boots making satisfactory stamping noises, as if she were an entire herd of people. The sunporch was small and lovely, papered in a beautiful yellow silk fabric printed with birds and flowers, with sun streaming in through the triple-glazed windows.

Oscar looked completely out of place in this pretty room. He had a plate of scrambled eggs and bacon in front of him. Another place was set across from him, a plate half-full of eggs and toast. A cup of coffee with lipstick on the rim. Christina tucked this information in the back of her mind to be reviewed later.

Oscar stared at Christina, scowling.

"Don't get up," Christina said, even though—or maybe because—she knew the older man had no intention of politely rising at her entrance.

"To what do I owe this surprise?" Oscar asked.

She pulled out a chair next to him and seated herself. "I'm throwing down a challenge."

Oscar leaned back in his chair and smiled. "You are, are you?"

She didn't let his arrogant attitude get to her. "If I'm right, Oscar Bittlesman, you're a betting man. I'm daring you to come work in my shed for just one hour. If you manage to stay for one full hour, I'll pay the increase in rent. But I'm betting that after an hour in that creaking, shaking, drafty rectangle of old wood, you'll see you've been charging too much and you *won't* raise the rent. You'll know you're lucky enough to get the rent you're getting now."

Oscar squinted at her. "You're aware, young lady, that you have no right to burst into my private home this way and sit at my table without invitation."

"I do know that. I'll leave the moment you accept my challenge."

He was frowning so hard he looked like a bulldog, but Christina caught the glint of interest in his eyes and held firm, glaring right back at him.

Oscar raised his chin defensively. "Fine. One o'clock tomorrow. One hour exactly and not a second more."

"I'll see you then." Christina didn't bother with any normal niceties. She stood up, turned her back on him, and strode back down the hall, head high, triumphant.

Janice was waiting by the front door.

"Thanks, Janice," Christina said. "You can return to your breakfast now."

"Christina, wait." Janice put her hand on Christina's arm and pulled her gently out onto the front porch, pulling the front door almost shut behind her. Janice looked especially pretty today in a simple green wool dress and cherry red earrings.

"Is something wrong?" Christina asked.

"Not wrong at all. But there's something I need you to know. Christina, Oscar is not simply my employer."

Christina grinned. "I thought you might have something going on with the old grouch. But why keep it secret, Janice? Does he enjoy treating you like the help?"

Janice bristled. "No, he does not! For your information, not that I want to share this with everyone, Oscar has asked me to marry him."

Christina gasped. "You're kidding."

Janice sniffed. "Well, that's a flattering remark."

"I'm sorry, Janice. I'm just so surprised. But why aren't you married?"

"Because I refused him. You know what it's like on this island. I have all my family and friends here. I have my routines and my way of life. I wouldn't change all that for the world. Who would want to be Mrs. Oscar Bittlesman?"

"But you'd be rich!"

"I *am* rich. I've spent half my life fixing my house to be exactly how I want it. It looks out over the moors, you know. I watch the deer and the hawks, I walk the paths and gather blueberries or beach plums and make jams and jellies. I've done that all my life. I took the job with Mr. Bittlesman because I needed the money. I've made some improvements on my house that I couldn't have afforded otherwise. I've made my mother comfortable and safe in the house, and that means a lot to me."

"But Oscar . . ."

"I never intended to fall in love with Oscar Bittlesman. You know, I've worked on and off for him for three years now. I have a nice little room off the kitchen in this house, and some nights I stay here, but most nights I go home. Oscar asked me as a special favor to be here constantly for the month of December because all his family would be here. I've moved my mother to my oldest daughter's house for this month."

"But, but," Christina stammered, "are you two . . . lovers?"

"Christina Antonioni, you know better than to ask such a personal question. You have no right to the answer. I care for Oscar—I love Oscar. And he loves me. We have wonderful times when we're together alone. You can't imagine how he changes when it's just Oscar and me." Janice smiled. "Oh, how we laugh."

"Didn't you feel awkward when we had dinner at this house and you cooked and served it but didn't eat with us?"

"Oh, no, honey. It's much more fun to be the fly on the wall. Oscar and I stayed up for hours picking apart the dinner conversation and laughing about it."

"Does Delia know? Or Andy? Or your friends?"

"I suppose Delia and Andy have an inkling, but Delia's too obsessed with her own life, and Andy's so good-natured, he doesn't intrude. As for my island friends, they have no idea. Why should they? I'm simply working as a housekeeper."

"I'm glad you told me this, Janice. It helps me see Oscar Bittlesman in a new light."

"I'm glad I told you, too. Maybe it will convince you that you could make a life with Andy Bittlesman."

Christina's shoulders slumped. "Janice, you know as well as anyone that I'm an island girl and Andy's a city guy. You just said you won't marry Oscar because you don't want to change your life."

"That's true. It's also true that you and Andy are a generation younger than Oscar and me. You're not as set in your ways. You and Andy are both changing—I can *see* you two changing. You can move toward each other. You can change each other. It won't be easy. I doubt if life with any Bittlesman can be easy, but who needs easy when they can have romantic?"

Christina laughed. "Janice, you're a wonder." She hugged the other woman tightly.

"So I can trust you not to tell anyone, especially my island friends, about my relationship with Oscar?"

"I'll keep your secret, Janice, I promise."

"Thank you." Janice opened the door and stepped inside. "Go on now, before we both freeze to death."

"Wait! Do you think Oscar will come to my shop tomorrow?"

"Honey, I don't interfere in Oscar's business and he doesn't interfere in mine. All I can say is that I wish you both well."

Christina couldn't stop smiling as she walked to her

car. *Oscar and Janice!* She understood and respected Janice's position. She could see how it would add to the fun for them both. Like a child's game of pretend.

Although it was too bad Christina couldn't have implored Janice to convince Oscar to be charitable about the rent. But Janice had said clearly that she didn't interfere in Oscar's business.

And anyway, maybe, Christina thought as she settled in her car, just *maybe* her plan would work and Oscar would be honorable about her challenge and not raise the rent.

But of course, maybe not. He was a cranky, money-mad old miser.

Should she tell the other Shedders about her bet? She thought about this as she parked her car and hurried down the brick sidewalk to the wharf. Should she get their hopes up when most likely Oscar wouldn't budge? Yes, because they would all be affected by the outcome.

She was fifteen minutes late opening her shop, but she didn't regret her impulsive action. Customers were waiting by her door, and as soon as she opened it, people poured in. She had no time to think about Oscar or Andy. No time to check her cellphone. Angels, elves, mermaids, pirates, and boats of every kind flew out of her store with happy customers.

During a lull, her store was empty while people were off having lunch. Christina changed the OPEN sign on her door to the WILL RETURN IN THIRTY MINUTES sign.

Andy tapped on the window. At the sight of him, her heart leapt.

"Come in, Andy," she said.

Andy stepped inside. He waited until Christina had locked the door before he spoke.

"You haven't returned any of my phone calls."

For a moment, Christina was speechless. Andy was so very much *there*, tall, handsome, and to her confusion, casually dressed in jeans and a down ski jacket. Oh, she realized, his good wool coat was probably still drying out. She flashed on the moment he'd raced into the geyser, his strong arms lifting her out and up, cuddling her close to him for warmth, striding into Mimi's.

And she flashed on Anastasiya standing there, watching . . . and giving Christina her warm fur hat.

"I'm sorry I didn't call you," Christina said. "Yesterday sort of knocked the stuffing out of me. I came back to the store in the afternoon, and it was a madhouse. When I got home, I pretty much collapsed."

"Are you okay now?"

"I'm fine. I didn't mean to be so histrionic, but the burst pipe was so shocking, so disorienting . . . and there you were with Anastasiya." She lowered her head. She couldn't meet his eyes. She didn't want to let him know how much it mattered.

"Did you listen to my messages?"

Christina nodded. "I did."

"So you know that Anastasiya and I aren't together in any way. She's engaged to Wonk. She and I are only friends, and nothing more. You believe me, don't you?"

"I . . . I do believe you." She wanted to rise up on her toes and kiss him passionately. Instead, she said haltingly,

"There's something else. You should know this. Maybe Oscar has already told you."

"I haven't spoken with him, except to say good morning. What has he done now?"

"It's what I've done."

"Really?"

"Really."

Andy folded his arms and leaned against a shelf. "Tell me."

"I barged into his house today and interrupted his breakfast. I dared him to stay in my shop for one full hour. If he remains for the entire hour, I'll pay the rent increase. Of course, I don't think I can, but that's another matter. I'm willing to bet he'll realize the rent shouldn't be increased."

"What did he say?"

"He's coming here tomorrow. At one o'clock."

Andy laughed. "Christina, I think you've just made him a very happy man. My father loves a challenge."

"I hope the temperature falls and the wind rises," Christina said. "The weather's been so mild, he'll think it's fine in here."

Andy put his arms around Christina's waist and pulled her toward him. "You make my temperature rise, you brilliant woman. I hope you know that whatever happens between you and my father tomorrow, it won't change how I feel about you. What I hope to have with you."

"What do you hope to have with me?" Christina asked quietly.

"A future. I hope to have you in my life forever. Christina, I *know*. Isn't it the same for you?"

Christina put her hands on Andy's chest. "I do know. But it's all happening so fast. It terrifies me, actually. How can I trust it?"

"You're right. It is happening fast. I guess we both have to trust it every day, and with each passing day, we'll be more certain."

Christina smiled. "You're such a romantic."

"You're the one who spends her days with mermaids and pirates," Andy said.

"They're make-believe," Christina whispered as Andy drew her closer.

"But you and I are real," Andy said. He cupped her head with his hand and brought his lips to her mouth.

Christina melted against him. She wrapped her arms around him and kissed him back with all the hope and desire and longing she'd been trying to deny. She felt like they were in the very center, the glowing warm heart of the world.

The sound of laughter came from just outside her windows.

"Andy. People are watching," she said. She pulled away and saw several teenage girls trying to stifle their giggles with their mittened hands.

"I know," Andy said. "You've got to open your store."

"I do." She couldn't stop looking at him.

"I'll go." Andy grinned. "Because if I stay, I'll take you right down onto this cold wooden floor so no one can see what we're doing."

"As tempting as that suggestion is, I'm afraid I've got to insist you leave."

"Fine. But look, I'm invited to a Christmas party at a friend's house tonight. I'd like to take you. Will you come with me?"

Christina hesitated.

"I promise, no serious kissing. But I might hold your hand."

She smiled. "You're irresistible. Yes, of course, I'd love to go to a party with you."

Outside, more people were peering in the window. Someone rapped on the door. She'd been closed for thirty minutes, not that that mattered to eager Christmas shoppers.

"I've got to open up." Christina told Andy.

"I'll go. And I'll pick you up tonight around six-thirty. Okay?"

"Okay."

Christina changed her sign, opened the door, and slipped back behind her counter as the customers flocked in. Andy waited politely for everyone to enter, then winked at Christina and left.

Again, the day flew by as shoppers swarmed into the store, searching for the perfect present. She had no time to close the shop for lunch, but during a lull, Christina managed to text Mimi, Jacob, and Harriet about the challenge she'd given Oscar.

Jacob texted back, *I'll keep my fingers crossed tomorrow.*

Mimi texted, *High five, darling!*

Harriet texted, *Wow, Christina, that's clever. I'm impressed.*

Wow, Christina thought, *a compliment from Harriet without an accompanying insult.*

Her phone buzzed again. *P.S.,* Harriet wrote, *Too bad you couldn't join us for lunch. I made a delicious chicken vegetable soup last night, brought it in a thermos, and shared it with Mimi and Jacob. And I flirted with Jacob. And I was nice! Jacob gave me the sweetest smile.*

Christina went warm all over. So Harriet had taken her advice and was softening. Maybe she'd even become pleasant!

Again, her phone buzzed. *P.P.S.,* Harriet texted, *but I still wish I knew if Jacob had money. If he even owns a condo on the island, that would clinch the matter for me.*

You're such a romantic, Christina texted back.

She started to put down her phone, when a thought struck her. *Harriet, get a copy of the town voter registration. We call it the Nosy Book. It will tell you where Jacob lives and what kind of neighborhood his house is in. Then you can check with the town clerk to see if he owns the house.*

Immediately Harriet texted back, *Christina, what a good idea! I think you're my best friend in the world!*

Well, that's a terrifying idea, Christina thought. *HEY!* her Inner Christina snapped. *Don't be so judgmental. You don't know what her life has been like, or who she's dated. Give her a break.*

"You're right," Christina said aloud. "I will."

At four o'clock, as darkness fell, customers were few and far between. By six o'clock, Christina had tidied her shop for the next day, prepared her bank bag, and locked her shop door. Business had been great, so she was feeling optimistic, although she stepped gingerly over the bricks as she made her way to her car. Her heart had been warmed by Andy's visit. She was no longer worried about the gorgeous Anastasiya, and she felt certain that whatever happened with Oscar and the rent, she and Andy were on their way to a serious relationship. Not only was she crazy sexually attracted to the man, she also just plain liked him. He was gorgeous, and he was nice. And he was making her believe that he felt the same way about her.

"What a difference a day makes," she hummed as she entered her house. Last night she'd been completely exhausted and downhearted. Tonight she was close to floating on air.

"Mittens, my good old feline friend!" She turned on the Christmas tree lights, sat on the sofa, and sweet-talked her cat until Mittens actually jumped in her lap and allowed her to pet her. "I've ignored you recently, haven't I?" she said, running her fingers through her silky fur. "But you know I love you, you gorgeous girl."

After Mittens decided she'd allowed Christina enough of her time and stalked off to the kitchen to wait indignantly to be fed, Christina fed the cat, took a long, hot shower, and dressed for the party. Andy had told her that their hosts were the Bishops, who lived on Hulbert Avenue. Christina had never met them, but she was looking forward to seeing their house.

She decided to wear her simple black dress and her grandmother's single strand of pearls with pearl eardrops. Once she would have been intimidated by people with a house on the harbor, but over the years she'd learned that it

was the young New York City rich who flaunted their
wealth, while the old-moneyed Yankees considered anything more than pearls ostentatious.

Besides, her few moments with Andy earlier in the day
had given Christina a glow no jewelry could outdo.

Andy knocked on her door at six-thirty. "I won't come
in," he said. "If I do, I'll kiss you, and then we'll never get to
the party."

"You're a wise man," Christina told him. She held his
arm and leaned against him as they walked to his car.

The house on Hulbert Avenue was meant for summer,
so the décor was casual, with huge paintings of seashells on
the walls. The Christmas decorations had been done pro-
fessionally. Everything was gold and silver and there were
frosted white branches and zillions of tiny white lights
everywhere.

"This is amazing," Christina told Andy. "It's like walking
into a different world."

The other guests were summer people. The women
were sleekly gorgeous, glittering with jewels, and the men
were tanned and muscular and loud, definitely alpha males.
Andy introduced Christina to some of his acquaintances,
and she said hello, then listened to conversations about
where everyone was flying for Christmas. Secretly, she tried
to remember names and which woman wore the emerald
earrings or diamond necklace so she could tell Harriet. Several of Andy's friends were friendly and funny and genu-
inely interested in what it must be like to live year-round
on the island. By the end of the evening, Christina told

several couples she hoped they would meet again. And she meant it.

Oscar and Delia arrived together. They made their way through the crowd to greet Andy and Christina. Delia's diamond earrings were so huge, Christina was surprised her earlobes didn't sag. Oscar looked distinguished in a red velvet jacket. And as Christina watched him pass through the room, she thought Oscar looked bored out of his mind. Several heavily bejeweled women raced up to him, kissing his cheek, batting their eyelashes. Oscar didn't look thrilled by the attention. *I bet*, Christina thought, *Oscar seriously misses Janice.*

It was the food that thrilled Christina. She had only one glass of champagne, but she couldn't resist the gourmet delicacies the caterer had prepared. Waiters passed by with trays of barbequed duck and lychee canapés, chorizo and prawn skewers, beef and mozzarella meatballs, polenta and prosciutto chips, thinly sliced sirloin twists on onion toast, and crumbed artichoke hearts with truffle aioli. If she'd had a pocket in her dress, she would have tucked a meatball wrapped in a napkin to take home to Mittens. But she didn't have a pocket, and she supposed that was a good thing.

After the party, as they drove toward her house, Christina asked Andy if Oscar had told him about her dare.

Andy laughed. "He pretends he's angry, but truly he's delighted. No one has had the courage to challenge him for a long time."

"It's going to be pretty close quarters in the shed,"

Christina said. "I've got one stool I sit on behind the counter. I'll let him use it. I'll tell him it's to keep him out of the way, but really I'm worried about him standing for a long time."

"Nonsense. Oscar Bittlesman could stand all day long if he had to."

Christina gave Andy a soft look. "I think you might be just a bit unrealistic about your father's general health."

Andy shook his head. "Why? He's only sixty-five. He has a gym in the basement and works out every day. Since he's lived on the island full-time, his health has actually improved. Cholesterol and blood pressure, down. Sense of humor, up."

"Let's hope he has a sense of humor tomorrow," Christina said.

When they reached her house, Andy kept the car running. He put his arm on the back of her seat. "This is what I'm going to do. I'm going to walk you to the door and say good night. I'm not going to kiss you because it's night and we're alone and if I kiss even your cheek, I won't be able to stop. I know you've got a big day tomorrow. I want you to be well rested, and *rest* is not something I want to do with you."

Christina smiled. "You're a gentleman."

"Gentleman, hell. I'm a saint!" Andy joked.

He walked her to the door, waited until she was safely inside, waved at her, and drove away.

snow was falling fast. She didn't think she'd have many customers today.

She checked her phone for missed messages. Nothing.
She took her coffee and toast into the living room and sank
onto the sofa to check out the weather on television. She
could find the same information on her phone, but she
liked to see the big picture on the big screen—was this a
long lasting winter storm? They'd had several in the past
few years.

And they had one now. Snow had fallen over the entire
Northeast, shutting down the MBTA in Boston and turning
the expressways into parking lots. The blizzard was barrel-
ing down from Canada, and it wasn't going to stop any time
soon. School was canceled all over Massachusetts, and in
Nantucket.

Flicking off the television, she looked out her window
at the street. It had been plowed, but her driveway was
deep in drifts. The blanket of white was beautiful, but a
giant hassle. Fortunately, she drove a four-wheel-drive Jeep
that could roar down a sandy beach and would take on the
snow easily.

But her shed would be cold.

She quickly showered and dressed for the day. As she
slipped into her silk underwear and her fleece shirt, she
wondered whether she should phone Oscar to tell him not
to try to come in today. But that might insult him. She'd let
him decide. She pulled on her fleece-lined boots and warmest gloves, shoved some extra gloves in her bag, and coated
her mouth with lip balm. Mittens was still asleep in the
middle of her bed.

16

Christina opened her eyes when her alarm clock chimed six-thirty. Mittens was curled next to her. Her bedroom curtains were closed, but the room seemed unusually bright.

"Mittens. It's cold in here, babe."

She sat up, pulled on her fluffy robe, and slid her feet into her slippers. At the window, she pulled her curtains back. She gasped.

Overnight, the island had become a winter wonderland. The ground was piled deep with drifts, the trees were straight from fairy tales, and the snow was still falling in great fat flakes.

"Oh, no." Christina hurried down to the kitchen, turne the heat up, and started boiling water for coffee. Usual falling snow lifted her spirits, but today Oscar was su posed to come to work.

Would Oscar Bittlesman actually come to the sh Would he even be able to get to the wharf? She knew DPW had probably plowed and sanded the roads, bu

"Tough life," she said to the cat, who did not bother to open even one eye.

She dumped dry food in the cat bowl, pulled on her down coat, and set out into the snowy day.

She let her Jeep warm up as she scraped the windows free of snow and ice. By the time she got back into it, she was covered with snow herself. She put the car in reverse. It shuddered for a moment, then bucked like a horse and roared its way through the snow to the street.

On the way to work, she passed children building snowmen and guys out with snowblowers and orange DPW trucks clearing streets. Not until she was down near the pier did Christina realize that in the few minutes she'd been out, the wind had picked up. When she was settled in her shop, she'd phone Jacob for a forecast. With all his equipment and knowledge, he was better than the Weather Channel for the faraway island of Nantucket.

Other shops along Main Street were open. Their lights cheered her immensely. It could feel lonely out on the wharf. And as she walked to her shed, she realized she'd be really lonely because the Hy-Line ferry wasn't running. That predicted a massive, long-term blizzard. Mimi's shop was open, and so were Jacob's and Harriet's, and someone had shoveled paths from the street down the wharf and right up to each shop door.

A path to her door had also been cleared. Probably Jacob had done it; he was so helpful that way. Inside, she turned on the lights and set her small electric heater to high. She kept her coat and hat on while she set up the cash register for the day. She doubted that she'd have

much foot traffic, but she set about tidying up her display
cases.

Her phone buzzed. "Do you think anyone will actually
shop today?" Harriet asked. "I'm freezing in here."

"I'm cold, too, but my heater will warm me up. You
should put on one of your cashmere caps and wrap a shawl
around you. You'll survive. By the way, Andy took me to a
party at the Bishops' house last night. I told several women
they really should check out your shop."

"That's so nice. Thanks, Christina! Oh! Must go!"

Through her window, Christina watched two women in
fur coats and hats make their way through the snow to
Nantucket Couture.

Several times that morning, people came by the toy
shop. Business wasn't brisk, but it was good enough. It was
only three days until Christmas so Christina and the other
Shedders stayed in their shops through lunch, not wanting
to risk losing a single customer.

The wind was rising. It drove the falling snow into fan-
ciful arabesques, and it whistled through the cracks in the
wooden walls of the sheds. Christina knew it would be a
struggle to make it through this cold day.

She assumed Oscar wouldn't show, but when she saw
a hunched male figure wearing a camel overcoat come
stomping through the snow, she smiled and hurried to open
the door for him.

"Oscar! You made it!"

Oscar powered through the door into the relative
warmth of the shop. "What, you thought a little snow would
keep me away?"

"Well, it's kind of wild out there. I'm impressed. Why don't you take that stool over there by the heater—"

"I don't need special treatment!" He started to take off his coat, thought again, and buttoned it back up.

"And I'm not giving you any. That's where Wink sits when she's sorting the small items back into their proper tubs. Like, the mermaids go here, and the mood rings go here—"

"For Pete's sake, I can figure it out, woman!"

"Then I'll leave you to it." Christina hid a smile as she turned away. Oscar clearly was angry that he'd come here, and he was going to be angrier once he tried to pick up those tiny whales and shells with his big fat fingers.

A moment later, the after-lunch rush began. Parents and children swarmed through the front door, sometimes making a beeline for the toy they knew they wanted, sometimes asking Christina for suggestions.

"I've got my entire family coming for Christmas," Maggie Merriweather told Christina. "So I've got gifts for my grandchildren, but there'll be about five or six cousins of various ages and I'd like to get a little something for them . . . I don't even know if they're boys or girls, and I don't want to spend a fortune, and I certainly don't want to have to return anything."

Christina smiled. Maggie's curly red hair had been shaped by the wind into an elfish swirl. "Why not get five of these," Christina said, showing Maggie the Surprise Bags. "They each cost five dollars, and there's a variety of cool things inside. Squishy squeezy animals and scented Silly Putty and wind-up penguins—they're always a hit.

Other customers have been more than satisfied with them."

"You're the answer to my prayers," Maggie said. "I'll take six."

"Put that back *now*, young man!" Oscar roared.

Christina whirled around. Oscar was standing over a little boy who gazed up at Oscar in terror.

"Is there a problem, Oscar?" Christina asked in her sweetest voice.

"This kid just stole a bag of marbles!" Oscar said.

"My son would never steal!"

It was Joyce Robinson, an obese and scrappy island woman known for getting drunk and fighting in bars. Oscar had met his match in her, but Christina didn't want an unpleasant scene in her shop.

"Your son put a bag of marbles in his pocket. Check it out. He's a little thief!" Oscar contended.

The little boy had tears in his eyes. Any moment now, he'd break into a full-on wail.

Christina hurried around the counter. "Oscar, I know Joyce and Billy. Billy would never steal. I'm sure he put them in his pocket so his hands were free for other things."

"Yeah, other things to put in his pockets," Oscar growled.

"Don't you dare talk about my son that way!" Joyce snapped. She grabbed her son's hand. "Come on. We're leaving!"

"Take the marbles out of his pocket first," Oscar demanded.

The boy's mouth quivered as he lifted the bag of marbles from his pocket.

"Would you like to buy these?" Christina asked gently.

"After the way that *man* treated us, you ought to give them to us," Joyce argued.

Aware that other customers were watching, Christina said politely, "I'm sorry. I can't do that."

"Didn't think so." Joyce sniffed. She took the marbles from her son, threw them at Christina, and dragged her son out the door, leaving it open for the snow to blow in.

"Sorry, everyone," Christina apologized, smiling at the other customers. "We're all emotional during the Christmas season."

People went back to choosing toys. Christina quietly led Oscar to the back of the store.

"Could you please check the price stickers on these boxes? They keep falling off. I got a bad batch."

"Busywork," Oscar grumbled.

"My shop is all busywork," Christina told him.

Returning to the counter, she rang up some customers and directed others to the lighthouses or tea sets or Legos. She had fifteen happy minutes before Oscar growled again.

"Don't buy that!" Oscar ordered. "Can't you see how cheesy it is?"

Christina nearly leapt over the counter, hurrying to get to the back.

"Oscar," she said, keeping her voice calm, "those little mermaid sets are handmade, one of a kind. The artisan lives on the island, and she takes exquisite care with her work."

"I can see that," the customer said. "I think my niece would love it."

"Yeah, if she likes being the odd one in her school," Oscar said.

"Oscar!" Christina said, only with the greatest self-control refraining from shouting.

"I suppose you're right," the customer said. She put the mermaid set back. She turned and hurried out of the store.

The door opened, and several more customers blew in. Because other people were around, Christina couldn't argue with Oscar about losing business for her. Thinking quickly, she said, "Why don't you run the register? I'll organize the shelves. You know how to use a register and a credit card machine, right?"

"Of course!" Oscar replied.

Oscar took his place at the register. Christina moved around the shop, replacing fallen toys, asking customers if she could help. For a while, everything ticked along pleasantly.

Then she heard a customer say, "I want a discount on this pirate ship. It has a ding in it."

"It's a *pirate* ship!" Oscar barked. "It's supposed to have a ding in it!"

Christina looked. The ship was one of the largest ones, its sails fastened with complicated rigging. It was an expensive item, one that few people would buy. Even with a discount, Christina would make a profit.

Christina slid silkily up to the customer. "I do agree with Oscar. Pirate ships should probably be even more battered than this one. Oh, look, it's only a slight dent. Oscar, give this gentleman a ten percent discount on this item."

"I will not!" Oscar said.

Christina took a deep breath. She didn't want to insult the man who owned the building her shop was in. But she couldn't let him act like a bully.

"Oscar, I think you need a breather. I have a thermos at the back of the store, over by the picnic baskets. Why don't you have a break, and I'll finish with this customer."

Oscar glared at her. Christina glared right back at him.

"I'd like to buy this fairy," a woman said, getting in line behind the pirate ship customer.

Reluctantly, Oscar left the counter and straggled to the back of the store. Christina gave the customer a ten percent discount and she rang up a lovely big amount on his credit card. She sold the fairy to the woman. In spite of the snow, customers continued to enter the shop, murmuring to themselves or their friends about what they needed to buy. Oscar stood with his back to Christina, arms folded over his chest, sulking.

Could this get worse? Christina wondered.

A large woman set a tiny birdhouse on the counter. "Do you gift wrap?"

Christina couldn't imagine what a package wrapped by Oscar would look like, and she couldn't leave him to tend to customers. "I'm sorry, we can't today," Christina told her. "I'll lay it in red tissue and put it in a bag for you." Turning her head, she asked politely, "Oscar, I've run out of small paper bags. There's a stack of them in the cupboard below the picnic baskets. Could you bring me some?"

Oscar muttered something incomprehensible, but did as he was told. As he approached the counter, he stopped short, looking offended. "You're going to put that little thing in a bag? You could easily put it in your enormous purse. Do you have any idea how much those bags cost?"

The large woman's eyes went wide. She backed away from the counter.

Christina had had it. "Don't mind him," she whispered to the woman. "Alzheimer's. I'm taking care of him today."

The customer smiled weakly. Christina carefully wrapped the birdhouse in tissue and tucked it into one of her paper bags.

"Thanks for coming," she said.

She took care of two other people, and then the shop was, for the first time in almost an hour, quiet.

"Oscar, your hour's almost up. Wouldn't you like to leave now? Go home and get warmed up?"

"Don't try to make me think I'm a weakling," Oscar said. "I'm staying my full hour!"

"Then maybe you'd just sit on that stool and, um"— Christina thought desperately for a task Oscar could do that would keep him from insulting her customers—"maybe keep an eye out for shoplifters?"

"Fine!" Oscar plumped himself down on the stool. After a moment, he said, "It's cold in here!"

"I'm glad you noticed," Christina said pleasantly.

Before Oscar could respond, more customers entered. For a good ten minutes, everything was calm.

Angie Rogers stepped into the store, her three-year-old twins, Spruce and Plum, on either side. "Now you be good and just look," she told them. "Mommy has to buy something."

As if hurled from a slingshot, the twins flew away from their mother, each one down a different aisle of the store.

"What can I help you find?" Christina asked. Angie was a very nice woman, but a bit of an airhead.

Before Angie could even respond, Spruce, the angelic-looking boy twin, made a putting sound and raced down the aisle with his hand straight out, knocking ships, dolls, small books, hand-carved whales, and innumerable rubber toys onto the floor.

"Stop that at once!" Oscar yelled.

"Oh, dear, what's he done now?" Angie asked, drifting to her son.

Spruce looked up at Oscar. Christina held her breath. Spruce must be terrified of the snarling old man.

With a grin, Spruce began jumping up and down, landing on the toys he'd scattered on the floor.

"What is your problem?" Oscar yelled at Angie. His face was a bright red, tending toward purple. "Stop your demon child at once, or I will!"

"Oscar," Christina said with quiet determination, "please stop. Angie, maybe you'd better come back when your children are with a babysitter."

Angie was crouched on the floor, picking up toys and tossing them into baskets.

"Mommy," Plum said, coming around the corner of the counter with a small stuffed puppy in her hands. "Can I have him?"

"Angie," Christina said, "don't worry about the mess. It won't take me long to fix it. And that puppy is eight dollars."

"Eight dollars?" Angie looked as if she'd been stabbed. "No, Plum, we can't get that puppy today." Taking both her children's hands, she dragged them out of the store, all three of them complaining loudly.

For a moment, the shop was empty. Christina stood watching out the window to see if other shoppers were headed her way and forcing herself to take deep breaths. When she knew she could keep from screaming at him, she turned to face Oscar.

He was picking up the toys Spruce had left. "That child's a menace."

Christina smiled. "Oscar, have you never worked in retail before?"

Oscar rose to his full height. "You know very well I'm the CEO of a multimillion-dollar investment firm. I have hundreds of employees."

"Yes, but that doesn't answer my question." She kept her eyes leveled at him. "In a small shop like this, it's necessary to make the customers feel welcome. You can't tell them what to do. They're not your employees."

"No, they're thieves and idiots!"

Christina put her hands on her hips. "They are *children*. They're hyper with excitement. Their parents' nerves are on edge, they're overwhelmed trying to put together a lovely warm holiday, and everyone's just a little bit crazy. The shop owner needs to be tolerant, and helpful, and kind."

"When I agreed to come here, I didn't sign up for a lecture," Oscar snarled.

"That's true," Christina agreed. "And fortunately for both of us, your hour is up."

Oscar checked his watch. "Humph." He was still wearing his wool cap and gloves. "I've been here an entire hour, you agree?"

"I agree." Her heart was in her throat when she asked, "And do you still believe the rent increase is justified?"

Oscar glared at her. "I do."

Christina couldn't believe her ears. She wanted to argue, to curse, to burst into long wailing sobs. But she held on to her dignity. "So you've stayed for a full hour. You've won the bet."

"Damn right I have!" Oscar stomped to the door and stormed out into the snow.

The shop was almost silent but the air shivered from the cold wind buffeting the walls. Christina forced herself to take a few calming breaths. It was only two o'clock. More customers would be coming. She would concentrate on them. She would smile and help them choose wonderful presents for their children.

But first, while the store was empty, she had to make a few phone calls.

She called Mimi, and then Jacob, and then Harriet. She told them that her dare hadn't worked. Oscar had stayed the entire hour. She'd promised him that if he could, she would pay the rent increase. She knew she couldn't do that, so after Christmas, she would close her shop for good.

The Shedders were kind. They all, even Harriet, thanked her for trying. They couldn't talk for long, because customers needed attention, and by the time Christina had told Harriet, her own store was filling with people.

The rest of the day flew by. More customers surged through the door. They needed *stocking stuffers!* Bags of marbles, miniature sailboats, rope bracelets, and sticker books flew into the toy shop bags and out the door. While that group was trying to get out, another group was shoving their way in. A woman in a fur coat bought a dozen wooden rainbow sailboats to be put at the top of each place setting for her dinner that night. A grandfather bought the large, jeweled pirate book for his grandson. A gang of schoolgirls about twelve years old shuffled in giggling and whispering, searching for something.

"Is there anything special you're looking for?" Christina asked.

This set off an especially explosive round of giggles.

"No, thank you," one of the girls said, and in a mass, like a giant amoeba, they squeezed back out into the cold.

A heart-stoppingly handsome man strode in. The shoulders of his black wool coat were coated with snow. "I wonder if you could help me. I'm looking for, um, well, what's your most expensive present?"

"For what age group?"

The man spotted a large box of Legos high on the top shelf. "I'll take that."

Christina picked up her folding step stool.

"Please don't trouble yourself. I can reach it. I'll take it down, if that's okay," the man said.

"Of course," Christina answered. "Thank you."

"This is a marvelous shop," the man said.

"Thank you," Christina repeated. "I quite like it myself." Her Inner Christina perked up: *You* quite *like it? What, all of a sudden you're British?*

As the man paid for the Legos and left, more customers entered the shop. Christina bagged small items, rang up the sales, reminded people how to use the chip on the credit card machine, replaced toys, and got so hot she took off her wool sweater and Christmas cap.

It was after five when the rush died down. She kept the store open after six, putting the shelves back in order, hoping a few more parents and kids would rush in. But dark had fallen, and the wind had risen. She gathered her things, locked the shop, and trudged to her Jeep.

17

Christina drove home, thinking the town had never looked more beautiful, all the buildings blanketed with snow, lights twinkling against the darkness like hope against despair. She held back her tears until the moment she walked into her house.

Mittens was there, meowing for her dinner. Christina picked up her beautiful friend and held her, burying her cold nose in the warmth of the cat's fur.

"Oh, Mittens, I've had such an awful day!" she cried.

Mittens wasn't interested in her drama. She slid out of her arms and raced toward the kitchen. Christina followed. She opened a can of food, set it in a bowl for the cat, and freshened her water bowl. Then she stood in the middle of her kitchen, still wearing her coat and hat and gloves, and tried to decide whether she wanted a drink of coffee or red wine.

She was too overwhelmed to decide. Why had she made such a stupid bet? She should have known that Oscar would have stayed in her shop for an hour if he'd had to cling to the shelves with his teeth. He was a tyrant. He didn't need the pitiful ten percent raise in rent, the raise that would make it impossible for the Shedders to keep their shops.

And how could she let the others down, and close her own business, and still keep any kind of loving relationship with Andy? She couldn't. She didn't even want to see Andy again, she never wanted to see *any* Bittlesman again, and that thought made her cry so hard she frightened the cat, whose fur stood on end as she raced from the room.

Christina's windows were full of darkness. She didn't turn on the Christmas tree lights, as if she was stubbornly rebelling against this season that was supposed to be so full of joy and instead was full of misery. It was an utterly childish *So there!* but she was too sad for the hope of light.

Why had she had to meet Andy? He was a man she could love, and now he was completely outside the range of possibilities. Sometimes it seemed like fate liked playing bitter jokes on people.

Her cellphone buzzed, but she ignored it. She trudged upstairs and ran a hot bath full of bubbles and perfume. She let her clothes fall right on the floor. She sank into the hot water with a sigh of relief.

Finally she was warm. She toweled off, pulled on her warmest fleece robe, and stepped into her fleece-lined leather slippers. She wasn't hungry—she was simply limp. When she merely thought of Andy Bittlesman, her heart jumped for joy. But when she merely thought of Oscar Bittlesman, her heart sank.

What now? It was too early to go to bed. Christina

supposed she could go back down to the living room and watch something on television. She would bet— *No more betting, ever!* dictated her Inner Christina. She *supposed* that the mushy movie *It's a Wonderful Life* would be playing on some channel. It would probably make her cry, but even *Zoolander* would make her cry tonight.

She dragged her miserable self downstairs, settled on the sofa, and picked up the remote.

Someone knocked on her front door. What now?

She heard giggling. It was only a little after eight.

Wearily, she trudged to the front door. She opened it to the surprising sight of the three other Shedders, Mimi, Jacob, and Harriet, all of them trying to squeeze into her house at once.

"Christina!" Mimi cried. "Let us in! We've got an idea!"

Christina couldn't help but laugh and hold the door open wide. "Come in, you crazy people."

As the others stood in the hall divesting themselves of coats, hats, mufflers, and gloves, Christina hurried into the living room to turn on the Christmas tree lights. All at once, her room sparkled with magic.

Mimi came into the room and dropped down on a chair. Jacob and Harriet sat on the sofa. Together.

"Can I get you all something to drink?" Christina thought this was a perfectly reasonable question, but it set the other three off in gales of laughter.

"No, no, darling," Mimi said, "just sit down and listen to us."

Warily, Christina perched on the edge of an armchair. "Okay."

"So," Jacob said, clearing his throat and sitting up very straight, "we three have been discussing how wrong we've been to let you carry the burden of dealing with the rent raise."

"Although it made sense since you've got an in with Andy Bittlesman," Harriet added.

"We decided we want to do our fair share," Jacob continued. "We've spent *hours* trying to figure out what we can do to change his mind."

Mimi couldn't keep quiet. "So we finally decided to go all Charles Dickens on him! We've called Elsa Fartherwaite, she's the organizing power behind the Nantucket Victorian Christmas Carolers—"

"They sang on Main Street during the Christmas Stroll," Jacob interjected.

"—and we asked her if we could borrow their Victorian costumes—"

"Because we're going to sing Christmas carols to Oscar at his house!" Harriet announced.

Christina studied the three faces before her, all so eager and hopeful and bright, like children waiting for the teacher to tell them they've given the right answer.

"What's more," Mimi continued, "we're going to give him presents from each of us."

"I'll give him a Ralph Lauren tie in red and white stripes," Harriet said.

"I'll give him a handsome brass-plated barometer," Jacob said.

"And I'll give him a Christmas sweater!" Mimi concluded.

"And you can give him the Great Point lighthouse model," Harriet told Christina.

Christina bit her lip. Were these adults sitting in her living room *serious*? Did they actually think a few songs badly sung—because she certainly didn't have a strong voice and she doubted if the others did—and a few presents would sway Oscar the Great's mind?

"I know what you're thinking," Mimi said. "It's not about the carols or the presents, although that should get him in the mood. It's about community. About being part of the island. Here we are, four people who live here year-round, and he's been pretty much isolated up there for three years—"

"Except for Janice," Christina reminded her.

"Exactly!" Mimi agreed. "And Janice is our trump card. I know she wants Oscar to feel part of the community, so after she hears our carols and sees our gifts, she'll soften him up."

Mimi, Jacob, and Harriet stared at Christina, breathlessly waiting for her response.

"I don't know what to say," Christina admitted.

"We've had a lot of ideas," Harriet told her. "I suggested that we kidnap Oscar and tell him we won't let him go unless he promises not to raise the rent."

"We decided against that," Mimi said.

"Really not in the Christmas spirit," Jacob added, winking at Harriet.

Christina's IC choked. *Jacob winked at Harriet?*

"The timing is good . . ." Christina said, thinking aloud. "He must feel triumphant after winning the bet today. On the other hand, he's not the kind of guy to get softened up by a few carols."

"Well, Christina," Harriet snapped, "why don't you give us a better idea? I mean, your plan with Oscar in the store didn't seem to change his mind. We're a little desperate here. Can you think of anything better?"

"No," Christina admitted. "I'm just afraid this, um, *wonderful* idea of yours won't work."

"We won't know until we've tried!" Mimi chirped.

"You're right, of course, Mimi." Christina had to smile at her friends' optimism. "I'm in. Let's do it."

"Hooray!" Mimi said.

"Actually," Jacob admitted, blushing as he spoke, "I have a decent baritone. I sang with my college glee club."

"I can sing," Christina said, "but not always on key."

The others laughed.

"Enthusiasm will be more important than technical accuracy," Mimi said.

"This is slightly . . . frightening," Christina admitted.

"I know," Jacob agreed. "Isn't that cool?"

Christina almost retorted that she'd had her share of scares this Christmas, thank you very much, but she was thrilled that Jacob was excited about trying something new.

"Very cool," Christina agreed. "Now. How many carols shall we sing, and what are they? And when shall we do this?"

"We should do this as soon as possible," Harriet said.

"We've discussed what carols we should sing," Mimi told her. "We've even tested a few."

"We don't want to be childish and silly, so 'Rudolph the Red-Nosed Reindeer' is out," Jacob added.

"We're thinking something knock-out beautiful," Mimi said. "Something so stirring Oscar's cold heart will melt."

"That might be too much to hope for," Christina cautioned them.

"We're thinking we'll start with 'In the Bleak Midwinter,'" Harriet said. "It's from a poem by Christina Rossetti, with beautiful music by Harold Darke."

"Oh, Harriet," Christina protested gently, "we don't want to try that. We'd absolutely ruin it. Let's think of something less ambitious. 'Silent Night,' maybe?"

Harriet pulled herself up straight, insulted. "I used to sing in college."

Mimi said quietly, "Christina, just listen."

Christina tried not to roll her eyes. "Sure."

Oh, brother, her Inner Christina said. *Plug your ears.*

Harriet folded her hands in her lap and began to sing.

"In the bleak midwinter, frosty wind made moan,
Earth stood hard as iron, water like a stone;
Snow had fallen, snow on snow on snow
In the bleak midwinter, long ago . . ."

Christina's jaw dropped. Harriet's voice was sweet and pure and full, a perfect angelic soprano. She was precisely on tune, each word winging from her mouth flawlessly. Christina's entire body broke out in goosebumps at the beauty of the sound.

Jacob joined in on the second stanza, holding his voice back, harmonizing with Harriet but never overwhelming her with his powerful baritone. His eyes rested on Harriet as they sang, as if he was hypnotized. As if he was in love.

Christina glanced at Mimi. Mimi was smiling smugly.

They arrived at the final stanza, their voices as shining as stars.

Tears spilled down Christina's face. She applauded, shaking her head in wonder.

"That was stunning. Harriet, I had no idea you could sing," she said.

"Oh, well, there are a lot of things you don't know about me," Harriet retorted, smiling triumphantly.

"What do you think now?" Mimi inquired with a contented smile.

"I think we absolutely should do it!" Christina said. "Harriet's voice would melt a heart of stone."

"So, Christina," Harriet asked, "would you like to solo on a carol?"

Her Inner Christina snorted: *You must be kidding.* "No, Harriet. I can scarcely sing on tune, and my voice is weak. Maybe we can sing a jolly song where the four of us can pitch in together, and you and Jacob can drown out me and Mimi." Christina turned to Mimi. "I'm assuming you can't sing like Harriet."

"I don't think many people in the world can sing like Harriet," Mimi replied.

"You have an excellent voice, too, Jacob," Christina told him.

"It's okay, but nothing like Harriet's. Still," Jacob said, smiling shyly at Harriet, "I think we make a harmonious pair."

"I couldn't agree more," Christina told him.

"Now," Mimi said, taking charge. "We've discussed what other carols to sing. We thought we'd start with 'White Christmas' as we approach Oscar's house. It's got three stanzas. We can sing them over again while we wait for the door to be opened and Oscar to see us. When he's there, Harriet can immediately begin with 'In the Bleak Midwinter.' After that, we'll change moods and sing 'Walking in a Winter Wonderland.' They're all grown-up songs, ones he's sure to know. People respond to music they know."

"Can't we have one childish song for Wink?" Christina asked.

"Good idea!" Mimi said.

"How about 'Away in a Manger'?" Jacob suggested.

"Let's have something fun," Christina told him. "'Frosty the Snowman'?"

"I like that," Harriet said.

Immediately Jacob agreed. "Me, too."

Christina glanced at Mimi. The other woman gave her a devilish smile. "We can put 'Frosty' in before 'Winter Wonderland.' And that's all. We should keep it short. People don't like to stand there smiling at carolers forever."

"I agree," Harriet said.

"I agree, too," said Jacob.

"Should we practice now?" Christina asked.

"Why not?" Jacob asked. He was clearly enjoying himself.

"Maybe we could all have a tiny glass of wine to wet our whistles?" Mimi suggested.

"Absolutely!" Christina rose and hurried into the kitchen.

"I'll help," Mimi said, following.

As they took glasses down from the cabinet and Christina popped open a bottle of prosecco, she whispered, "Looks like we've got a romance going on."

Mimi whispered back, "Christmas magic."

They carried the bubbling drinks back to the living room. For the next hour, they sang and revised and sang and always Harriet's sweet pure soprano spiraled high, leading the way.

When the three other carolers left, Christina went to bed.

With her phone in her hand.

She waited ten minutes, enough time for Mimi to get home, then tapped Mimi's number.

"Mimi," Christina said as soon as her friend answered, "what's going on with Harriet and Jacob?"

"Isn't it wonderful? Harriet brought us hot soup for lunch yesterday and Jacob asked Harriet out to dinner and I'd bet my bottom dollar they're in love."

"Christmas magic," Christina agreed.

When they said goodbye, she snuggled down into her covers, feeling a bit like a Secret Santa.

18

Christina woke up hungry. She sat up, threw off the covers . . . and yesterday evening's events came flooding back into her mind. Today she felt much more optimistic about life in general. *That's what singing Christmas carols can do,* she thought, and she was grateful for it.

Downstairs, she started the coffee brewing and checked her cellphone while she waited. Louise had called twice. So had Jacob. And Mimi.

And Andy.

Her optimistic mood sank, not completely, but slightly, so she reminded herself that she was hungry and set about making scrambled eggs with cheese and bacon and toast with slabs of butter and cherry jam. Simply working in the kitchen lifted her mood. She remembered all the times she'd been downhearted as a child, and her mother had said, "Oh, you're just hungry. Find something good to eat."

It was a wonder she didn't weigh three hundred pounds.

On the other hand, her mother's advice had almost always worked.

The coffee and breakfast filled her with energy for the day. It would be super busy, and she had to get in early to do the books for yesterday, which she hadn't gotten done because of the Oscar incident. Outside her kitchen window, she saw that snow layered everything in a thick cover of sparkling white. The wind had stopped howling and the sun was out, making the icicles dangling from the trees shimmer like prisms.

She flicked on the radio and sang along to the Christmas carols as she made a thermos of hot coffee and a quick and easy peanut butter and jelly sandwich. Upstairs, she dressed in her warmest clothes and pulled a wide woolen headband over her hair. She pinned a snowman to the headband, slipped on her dangling Christmas earrings, and for extra protection against the cold, she tied a wool scarf around her neck.

Ready to set out for her shop, she paused. She hadn't returned anyone's calls. Well, she'd see Mimi and Jacob on the wharf, and Louise would assume Christina was busy and overwhelmed with her store, which was the truth.

She drove carefully to the wharf. The sun was coming out from behind puffy white clouds. Houses and shops wore sparkling white hats and the trees were frosted with glitter. Christina smiled, remembering what Wink had said when Christina asked her what she wanted for Christmas.

"I want a makeup kit and a sparkly slime-making kit!" the little girl had declared.

And that's what it was to be nine, Christina thought, poised between childhood and tween-hood. Nine years old was such a perfect time. It was too bad it couldn't last for three or four years.

She slid her Jeep into a parking place across from the A&P and stepped out into the snow. The sun was almost completely out now, and it sparked off the windows and snowdrifts like scattered diamonds. The harbor water was a calm, innocent blue, as if it hadn't been a black explosive cauldron last night.

Really, the little shops, with their Christmas wreaths sprinkled with snow and their windows bright with decorations, seemed like a vision from a fairy tale—one with a happy ending.

Christina stopped, got out her phone, and snapped some shots. No one else was open yet, and she was early, wanting to catch up on the work she hadn't done yesterday.

She opened her shop door and stepped in to what felt like a refrigerator. She turned on the lights and the electric heater. Soon the place would be tolerably warm. She sat on her stool as close to the heater as she could get, and put together the checks and cash for a bank deposit. She had done well yesterday, and she'd do well today, she knew.

She was walking around her shop, straightening, organizing, turning dolls to face front, when her cell buzzed.

"Hi, Delia," she said happily. "How's Oscar?"

"He's just like he always is. I'm calling to tell you that Wink might stop in to see you today. She says she misses you." Delia's voice was completely neutral, not her usual

snobby pinched-nose cheese-grater sound, but not especially friendly, either.

"Oh." Wink missed her? Christina couldn't speak for
the lump in her throat.

"Okay, then. That's all."

"Merry Christmas!" Christina chirped.

"Merry Christmas," Delia replied, and somehow she
made the words sound like "whatever."

Christina went back to her organizing with a heavy
heart. She missed Wink's company. Really, she'd let herself
get too attached to the child, a foolish thing to do. Now, not
only would she lose Wink's friendship, but she would lose
her shop, too.

She had to start thinking of alternatives for her life. Her
shop, and all the Shedders' shops, were geared toward the
tourists visiting Nantucket for a day or two. These people
didn't have cars, and didn't need them. The town was com-
pact and easy to walk around. For that reason, rent in any
space in town was exorbitant. Maybe she and Mimi and the
others could find a space they could all share . . .

Someone tapped on the door. Surprised, Christina saw
that it was nine o'clock. She hurried to let the customer in,
and for the rest of the morning she was ringing up sales and
couldn't think about anything else.

At noon, the rush of customers slowed, then vanished.
Everyone treasured hot lunches on this cold day. Christina
was just about to call Mimi to see if the Shedders were having lunch at her shop when she saw Andy walking to her
door.

"Merry Christmas, Andy," she said, letting him in, locking the door behind him, and changing the small plastic OPEN sign in the window for the WILL RETURN IN THIRTY MINUTES one.

"Merry Christmas, Christina."

Before she could think twice, Andy took her in his arms and kissed her quite thoroughly.

"Wow!" she said when they came up for air. "You're in a fine mood today!"

Andy grinned. "I'm always in a fine mood when I'm with you, Christina. But wait," he joked. "There's more!"

He reached into his breast pocket and brought out an envelope.

"My father wants me to give this to you."

Christina took a step back. "Is he suing me?"

Andy laughed. "Just the opposite. Open it!"

Warily, Christina slit open the envelope and took out two crisp sheets of paper.

The first one was an official letter from Oscar, stamped by a notary public.

The second sheet was the deed to her shed.

Christina gasped. She read Oscar's letter carefully.

"Read it out loud," Andy urged.

"Okay. 'I, Oscar Ferdinand Bittlesman, do hereby freely and without compulsion, give the deed and title to Building 36A to Christina Antonioni.'"

Christina stopped reading and simply stood there, staring at the paper.

"Well?" Andy asked. "Isn't that great?"

Christina straightened her shoulders and stared Andy

in the eyes. "I can't accept this, Andy." She handed the papers back to him.

"I don't understand."

"Andy, I can't take ownership of this shed and let my friends lose theirs. They can't pay ten percent more in rent. It wouldn't be right." She blinked back tears.

"I'm sorry," Andy said. "Father thought this would please you."

"I'm sorry I'm so prickly," Christina answered. "Look, I have to focus on my shop now. I need some time to think."

"Can I see you tonight?"

Tonight the Shedders were caroling Oscar. "Not tonight, Andy. I've got plans." She smiled, thinking of her secret. "Although, it's just possible that you will see me tonight."

"I'm confused," Andy said.

"That makes two of us," Christina told him. She stepped back. "I'm sorry, but I see customers headed this way."

"Will you call me?" Andy asked.

"You'll definitely hear from me tonight," Christina promised.

She changed the sign again and opened the door. Two women, chatting excitedly about Christmas Eve, swept in. Andy squeezed Christina's hand tight, kissed her gently on her cheek, and left.

The store was stuffed with shoppers. Christina rang up sales and handed out credit card receipts as fast as she could. She felt like a racehorse on the last length of the track. Outside, the sun was sinking and the sky was dimming to gray.

"Christina!"

Christina looked down and saw Wink standing in front of the counter.

"Hi, sweetie!" Christina wanted to rush around the counter and seize the little girl and hug her long and hard. "Do you want to buy something?"

"Uncle Andy says you're mad at us. I don't want you to be mad at us, Christina."

All at once, every eye in the shop was on Christina. Christina knew she couldn't get around the counter to Wink without squeezing herself past people bulging in quilted parkas. She leaned over the counter and said, as quietly as she could, "Oh, dear, Wink, of course I'm not mad at you. I love you, sweetheart. Listen, I'll call you, tonight or tomorrow, and maybe after Christmas we can do something together in town, go to the library, maybe the ice skating rink . . ."

"But what about Christmas?" Wink asked. Tears were gleaming in her eyes. "I have to see you on Christmas! I have a gift for you."

Now half her customers were watching this little drama with fascination and the other half were loudly clearing their throats and coughing, making it known they wanted to buy their presents and leave.

"I'll call you, Wink. We'll work something out. I promise." She almost said: *We have a surprise for you and your family. I'll see you tonight.* But she knew the importance of secrets, so she kept quiet.

Wink nodded. "And you're not mad at us."

"I'm not mad at you," Christina told the little girl, and it was true, she wasn't mad at Wink.

"Okay!" Wink threaded herself between the shoppers and left the shop. Christina could see the child skipping along the snowy path. Her heart was lighter.

"Who's next?" she asked, ready to ring up the next sale.

19

Christina stood in front of the full-length mirror in Elsa Fartherwaite's guest bedroom and curtseyed.

"No, no, you can't do that," Mimi said. "You've got a green velvet cape with a white fur hood. People curtsey to *you*."

"No one curtseys," Harriet announced. "We're all aristocrats."

"I certainly am," Jacob said, lifting his black silk tall hat and bowing.

"Here," Mimi directed. "Let's all squeeze in together in front of the mirror."

They obeyed, and smiled at the sight.

Harriet was the most beautiful, with a wreath of holly and ivy in her blond hair. She wore a red silk gown that managed to elevate her marvelous breasts upward. Over that, but not completely over that, she wore a red velvet cloak.

Next to her, and unabashedly looking sideways down Harriet's magnificent bosom, stood Jacob, wearing a black tailcoat with a red vest and a white bow tie and a very tall black hat.

Next to Jacob stood Christina, who knew she looked fabulous in her green velvet cape with the white hood and matching white fur muff. She'd swept her long brown curls up and tied them with red and green silk ribbons, letting the ribbons and some of her hair curl down around her face.

The truth is, her Inner Christina whispered, *you're more beautiful than Harriet*.

Stop that, Christina whispered back. *Be good!*

By far the most sensational was Mimi, clad in a purple velvet cape embellished with black embroidery and an enormous purple hat ornamented with fake flowers and jewels and black bows and even a cluster of purple grapes.

"These costumes really set the mood, don't they?" Mimi said. "I swear I'm going to walk out and find a horse and carriage waiting for us beneath the gaslight lamps."

"Okay," Jacob said, "it's time to get going."

"Now I'm nervous," Christina confessed.

"Don't be," Harriet assured her. "I'll be there."

With all their capes and skirts bustling, they crowded out into Elsa's hall.

Mimi, with the other three behind her, stuck her head into Elsa's living room. Elsa, in her seventies and widowed, sat in a wingback chair in front of the fireplace.

"We're ready to go, Elsa!"

Elsa clapped her hands together. "You all look beautiful! Have fun!"

Mimi directed the others to her SUV. "I'm driving. Christina, you ride shotgun. Harriet and Jacob can share the backseat." Her mouth quirked up in a mischievous grin.

Once they were settled in, Mimi handed Christina a bag of throat lozenges. "Pass them around," she said. "Can't hurt."

It took only ten minutes to drive up the winding road to the cliff and Oscar Bittlesman's house.

A BMW was parked in the driveway. All the lights were on downstairs and a few upstairs, too.

"I guess they don't worry about electric bills," Harriet grumbled.

"Now, now," Mimi cautioned. "No negative feelings. We're here to entertain and delight."

"I'm going to drive on a house or two and park so it doesn't look like we've come specifically to them." Mimi slowly drove along. She parked the car. She asked, "Ready? Do you all have your presents?"

"I'm terrified," Christina said.

"Deep breaths," Jacob told them. "Let's all do a scale together to loosen our throats."

Mimi raised her hand to start them off. They raced up and down the scale. "Maybe more gently, my dears. We'll start singing 'White Christmas' when we reach the end of their drive, and we'll keep it up until they open the door. Once Oscar's there, Harriet and Jacob can sing their duet."

Christina's heart thudded away as they walked, singing, up the drive and onto the Bittlesmans' porch. She was glad she had the others with her, but that was why she was so nervous. It was one thing for Oscar to be mean to her, but she didn't want him to insult her friends.

They continued singing as they stood on the porch. And continued. Maybe, Christina thought, maybe they were all watching television and couldn't hear the carolers.

Finally, the door opened.

"Oh, my! Carolers!" Janice was there in a blue dress with an apron over it. She smiled at the quartet. "Let me get the others!"

They sang the last verse of "White Christmas" for the fourteenth time, and then Janice returned with Oscar and Wink in tow. Delia stood behind Wink, rolling her eyes. Andy showed up, grinning with delight.

Wink clapped her hands and jumped up and down at the sight of the carolers.

Oscar stared at them grimly, as if they were another task to finish.

Without a moment's hesitation, Harriet began to sing.

"In the bleak midwinter, frosty wind made moan, earth stood hard as iron, water like a stone."

Janice gasped and placed both hands over her heart. Wink clasped her hands to her face in wonder. Andy's eyes lit up in surprise. Oscar didn't change expression, but at least he didn't walk away.

Harriet sang easily, purely, her voice rich even in the highest notes. Jacob's quiet baritone gave solemnity to the song.

Christina's eyes filled with tears and the tears spilled over. What a gift Harriet had, and what a gift she was giving.

After Harriet sang the final line—"I give him—Give my heart"—Wink asked, her voice trembling, "Are you an angel?"

"Yes," Jacob said. "Yes, she is."

Oh boy, Christina's IC whispered, *has Jacob got it bad*.

"Here's a song for you, Wink," Mimi announced.

The group launched into "Frosty the Snowman," which delighted Wink so much she laughed and clapped. They segued right into "Winter Wonderland."

Janice, Andy, and Wink applauded. Oscar stood unmoved.

Mimi said, "And, Oscar, since the older of us often miss out on Santa Claus, we've each brought you a gift."

"I'll put them under the tree!" Wink cried.

The Shedders handed their carefully wrapped packages to Wink, who raced away to put them under the tree.

"Merry Christmas!" the Shedders cried.

"Merry Christmas!" Janice replied.

"Merry Christmas!" Andy replied.

Oscar walked away.

The quartet was silent as they returned to Mimi's car. They remained silent until they were down in the town.

"Oscar didn't seem to appreciate it," Harriet said sadly.

"Oh, you never know with someone like him," Christina hurried to assure the other woman. "He probably didn't crack a smile when his first child was born."

"Wink loved us, and Janice almost cried," Mimi reminded them.

"Well, I hate him," Harriet announced darkly. "He's mean and he's heartless."

"I hate him, too," Jacob said loyally.

They returned to Elsa's house and divested themselves of their costumes. Jacob changed into street clothes in the bathroom, leaving the three women to change in the bedroom. They hung the capes tidily in the wardrobe filled with Christmas outfits. Mimi returned her extravagant hat to the hat cupboard, and Christina could tell she regretted having to leave it behind.

Maybe she'd make Mimi a fabulous hat for next Christmas. No, for Easter! That would be a fun project.

Elsa was waiting in the hallway. "Would you all like a little sip of sherry?" Seeing their faces, she added, "Or maybe a spiked eggnog?"

"No, thanks," Mimi said. "We've all got to get home. We have to work tomorrow and I must say we're exhausted. I don't know how you carolers manage to sing all during the Stroll."

"Oh, we're used to it," Elsa said, with a wave of her hand.

"Well, we're very grateful for the loan of the costumes," Christina told Elsa.

The other three chimed in. Elsa opened the door and the four left, returning to the cold outdoors. Christina had driven there in her own car, and Jacob had driven Harriet, so they all said goodbye and wished each other "Merry Christmas," but their voices weren't very merry at all.

As Christina waited for her Jeep to warm up, she said, "I hate him, too."

She drove to her house, feeling absolutely dismal. The Shedders hadn't succeeded in pleasing Oscar. Christina wondered if anything other than money made him smile.

Well, Wink did.

Back at her house, cozy in flannel pajamas, Christina collapsed on her bed just as her phone buzzed.

"How did it go?" Louise asked.

It brightened her mood to hear her friend's voice. Louise consoled her for the discouraging evening, then went on to discuss her own Christmas chaos, and to ask if she'd heard that Bea Montgomery fell in the snow, broke an ankle, and was having surgery at Mass General.

"Poor Bea! This is turning into an absolutely *calamitous* Christmas season."

Louise assured her, "You're just having the Pre-Christmas Crazies. That's when all kids become little monsters a few days before Christmas. It's the waiting that builds the tension. We adults probably have some version of it."

"I think you're right, Louise," Christina said. "Talking to you is as good as two glasses of wine."

"You can phone Dr. Louise anytime," Louise teased. "Now, give me the scoop about Andy."

"It's confusing," Christina warned.

"I can handle it," Louise said.

They talked about Andy Bittlesman, and what Christina felt about him (mad crazy lust and love) and what Louise had heard about him (a solid stand-up good guy) and where Anastasiya Belousova was (in Paris, with Wonk; Louise had googled) and what had convinced Louise that her boyfriend, now husband, had really loved her (he named his boat *Louise*) and what it would take for Andy to convince Christina he loved her (was it too soon to tell?). They talked about Harriet and Jacob and how Louise's daughter, Dora, adored Wink, and finally Christina said, "I've got to go to bed. Tomorrow's a big day in my shop. It's Christmas Eve!"

20

The late afternoon on Christmas Eve was always profitable for Christina because so many people came rushing in at the last moment, having only just remembered a child on their list. These shoppers usually wanted something that would be a keepsake of the island for a child, and Christina sold out of rainbow sailboats and anything mermaid or whale.

The last customer finally left. Christina took a moment to lean on her counter and take a deep breath. She needed to slow down. She felt as if she'd been in an emotional popcorn popper today.

When she looked up, she saw the tall, handsome man who'd bought the Legos walking toward her store.

He was carrying the box of Legos.

Delia Bittlesman Lombard was walking next to him.

And here we have it, Christina thought, *the perfect end to this topsy-turvy day.* Delia was making the man return the Legos. The most expensive item in her shop. A huge financial loss for Christina's Toy Shop.

Hurry up! her Inner Christina shouted. *Turn off the lights! Lock the door! Don't let them in!*

Her pride wouldn't let her do that. She waited in misery as the couple came closer, closer, and then there they were, pushing open her door and stepping into her shop, stamping snow off their feet.

"Hi, Delia," Christina greeted the other woman, forcing herself to smile.

"Hi, Christina," Delia said, and *she* smiled, too, a great big, genuine smile.

Christina stared.

"Christina," Delia continued, "I'd like you to meet my husband, Jeff. Jeff, this is the Christina Wink's been telling you all about."

The big, handsome man in his designer coat (Harriet would hyperventilate) came across the room and held out his hand. "Hello, Christina."

"Hello, Jeff," Christina responded. She pulled herself together. "You have a wonderful daughter."

"That's true. We do." He turned and gave Delia a significant look.

Delia came to stand next to Jeff. "And we're giving her the best Christmas present of all. We're back together. We're not getting divorced! Jeff will be here for Christmas."

Tears came into Christina's eyes. "How wonderful for Wink."

"And for us," Jeff said, squeezing his wife close to him.

"But we have a problem," Delia cooed.

Great, Inner Christina moaned. *Now what?*

"How can I help?" Christina asked.

Jeff set the huge box of Legos on the counter. "I bought this because it's the biggest thing in the shop. Delia tells me Wink doesn't want the biggest thing in the shop."

"That's right," Delia chimed in. "Wink would like the most interactive thing in the shop."

"So what would you suggest, Christina?" Jeff asked.

"Why not surprise her with some board games she can play with her parents?" Christina suggested. She led them to the shelves stocked with board games. "For example," she said, pointing to each game as she spoke, "Wink might like Hey, Pa! There's a Goat on the Roof, or Qwirkle, or Carcassonne." When Delia and Jeff didn't respond, Christina continued, "We've also got Rummikub and Sequence and Llama Drama and all these old favorites like Scrabble Junior and Twister and Clue."

"They look great!" Jeff said. "We'll take them!"

Christina blinked. "Which ones?"

"All of them," Jeff said.

"Plus any others you think Wink would like," Delia added. Seeing Christina's hesitation, she explained, "We only have Monopoly at Father's house. We really need to stock up."

"Well, yes, of course," Christina said breathlessly. "First, let me credit you for the return of the Lego set. Then we'll start on the games you'd like to buy."

It took almost half an hour to ring up the game boxes and put them into Christina's Toy Shop bags.

When they were finished, Christina said, "That will be four hundred and twenty-three dollars."

"Oh," Delia said, tugging Jeff's hand, "let's get her the

lighthouses and ferries, too. She can take those back to New York to remind her of the island."

The total amount of their purchases rose considerably, but Jeff Lombard's credit card zipped its acceptance immediately.

"Thank you, Christina," Delia said. "You were so helpful."

"Yes, thank you," Jeff added.

"Thank *you*," Christina said weakly.

Both Delia and her husband had their arms full of packages. Christina hurried to open the shop door for them.

"Merry Christmas," Christina said as they left.

"Merry Christmas!" they answered.

As Delia went out the door, she turned and winked at Christina.

Christina surveyed the long snow-covered wharf. All the other shops were closed. She'd had a very successful business day, but as she turned the sign to CLOSED, locked her door, and leaned against it, she was exhausted, body and soul. Money was not everything, and on Christmas Eve, she longed to be with people she loved.

She checked her phone. Mimi had called to wish her Merry Christmas and to say she was closing her shop and heading home.

Janice had called and asked Christina to return the call as soon as possible.

Christina sighed. Now what? She might as well get it out of the way. Reluctantly, she tapped "Call."

"Oh, um, hang on," Janice said, sounding overwhelmed. "I'm just . . . I'll just . . ."

Christina waited.

When Janice spoke again, she sounded as if she was shut in a closet. "Christina, sorry, I'm just cooking and everyone's around and I don't mean to interfere but I want you and your friends to know that Oscar's wife also sang soprano. She was extremely talented and often soloed in their church choir. Oscar was overcome with emotion hearing Harriet sing—well, we all were, really. She was amazing. But Oscar was so deeply touched that when you all left, he shut himself in his study for hours."

"Oh, Janice, I had no idea. We certainly didn't intend to upset him."

"I think it was good for you all to come. He won't talk about it, but I can tell the carols broke through his reserve. Only a little, but still . . ."

"Thanks for telling me, Janice—"

"No, no, I'm coming, don't put it in the oven yet!" Janice called. The phone went blank.

Christina smiled, warmed by Janice's message. She'd call the others tonight—or maybe not. It was Christmas Eve. Janice was obviously surrounded by the family as she made dinner. Mimi would be with her family. Jacob and Harriet were probably together.

And she hadn't heard from Andy.

Should she phone him? When she refused Oscar's offer yesterday, maybe Andy had become discouraged with her. Disenchanted.

Returning to her spot behind the counter, Christina gathered together her bank bag and her credit card machine and her stacks of signed receipts. She was too tired to deal with all this right now. She wanted to sit down with a nice glass of wine and . . . and what? Sit alone in her living room, crying in front of Mittens?

Her friends often had Christmas Eve parties, but they started and ended early so the children could wind down and be put to bed.

In the past, whether she'd been dating or not, she'd always spent Christmas Eve and Christmas Day with her parents. They always attended what was called the midnight service at the church. Actually, it started at ten-thirty and ended at midnight. The music was glorious. She could go by herself, but she thought she wouldn't have the energy. And probably she'd embarrass herself by weeping. Tonight of all nights, she missed her parents.

Right now, she was too profoundly sad to cry. As she pulled on her coat, hat, and gloves, and hefted her purse and bank bag full of money, she felt heavy. Her heart was full of lead. She locked the shop door and trudged over the snowy path to the street and her Jeep, which was, of course, ice cold. She sat dejectedly warming up the car.

After a while, she listlessly drove home, past the shops with gorgeous decorations and the houses with their windows twinkling with lights.

She turned onto her street. Cars were parked nose to nose on both sides. Someone was having a party.

She turned into her driveway and gasped.

From *her* windows, light beamed. The Christmas tree twinkled cheerfully from her front window. Smoke spiraled from the chimney—someone had made a fire. Who? Mimi? Louise? Although she always locked her shop, she seldom locked her house. Most island people never locked their doors. Then she saw her front door open.

Wink peeked out. "Come in, Christina!"

Laughing, Christina stepped out of her car and hurried along the path that someone had shoveled to her house.

Wink held the door open wide. "Surprise!"

Christina stepped into the bright warmth, and her heart swelled with joy.

She could hear chatter and laughter and she smelled something wonderful cooking.

"Come on!" Wink said, tugging on Christina's hand. "We're all in the kitchen!"

And they were. All in the kitchen.

Including Delia and Jeff.

Delia, Jeff, Andy, and Oscar were seated at the kitchen table with homemade cookies shaped like stars, wreaths, reindeer, and Santa in front of them. Several bowls of icing were in service as they decorated the cookies.

"Don't eat the silver balls," Wink warned her. "They crack your teeth."

Delia, holding a knife covered with red icing, looked up. "Nice to see you again, Christina."

Christina grinned. "Nice to see you, Delia. And you, Jeff."

"He's my daddy!" Wink crowed. "He's spending Christmas with us. He and my mommy love each other!"

"Oh!" Would she ever get used to the way Wink blurted out information? "How nice!"

Oscar, a half-eaten cookie in his hand, looked up.

"Merry Christmas," he rumbled, and he almost sounded as if he meant it.

Andy rose from the table. "Merry Christmas. Let me take your coat and hang it up. And I'll put your bags and purse on the top shelf of the closet, okay?"

"Okay." Christina was too stunned to say more.

Janice was at the stove, stirring a rich stew of chicken and vegetables. She glanced over her shoulder. "Merry Christmas, Christina."

"Oh, Janice," Christina said, startled into action. "You shouldn't be cooking. Let me help."

Janice smiled a beautiful smile. "No worries, Christina. Oscar wants me to make his traditional Christmas Eve dinner. I like doing it." She winked at Christina.

"Sit down," Delia said. "I'll pour you a glass of wine. And here—" Delia shoved a platter toward Christina. "I made some munchies."

"Take my chair, Christina," Wink said. "I'll sit on Daddy's lap."

As if her legs had gone limp, Christina almost fell into the chair.

Andy returned from the hall. "We've set the dining room table, too. Wait till you see it."

"We'll eat in about ten minutes," Janice said.

"Here," Delia said, handing Christina a glass of wine.

"Thank you," Christina said, surprised her voice would work. She took a sip of the red wine. Its warmth curled down inside her and her frozen body stirred to life.

"Thank you all," she said, glancing at every person in

the room. "I'm so surprised! I can hardly believe this is real."

Wink chirped, "That's because you think you're the only one who can be generous. That's what Grandfather says."

Christina frowned in surprise. *Actually*, her IC muttered, *he's not completely wrong.*

Oscar cleared his throat. He looked at Christina. "Never say anything in front of this child that you don't want repeated."

"I think we can dress the salad now," Janice said.

"No, don't get up," Delia told Christina. "I know perfectly well how to toss a salad with olive oil and vinegar."

Andy took the chair next to Christina. "You're so quiet. Tired?"

"In a state of shock," Christina said.

"How was business?" Oscar asked.

"Crazy," Christina told him.

"Do you have problems with shoplifters?" Oscar asked.

"Not today, usually, because Christmas Eve is mostly adults. The shoplifters in my shop tend to be children, who snatch a marble or a sticker book, something they can easily palm and slide into a pocket." Christina didn't glance Wink's way as she spoke. She took a big hit of wine. She thought she might be hallucinating, all these people in her house and Oscar actually smiling.

The dining room table was set with her grandmother's snow-white linen tablecloth and her parents' good china, sterling silver, and cloth napkins. In the middle of the table was a long, low arrangement of white lilies, red carnations, and holly. Andy escorted his father to the head of the table and seated Christina at what her parents always called "the other head of the table." Janice brought the tureen of chicken stew to the table and Delia carried in the salad. Janice went off and returned with warm homemade rolls.

"What a feast!" Christina said. "Thank you, Janice."

"Uncle Andy and I picked out the flowers!" Wink said.

"You did a great job," Christina told her.

As they ate, Janice and Christina reminisced about past Christmases, when not so many people lived on the island, and there were no fast ferries.

"And," Janice said, "if you can imagine, no catalogs except Sears! The only way we could order something was to go out the airport road and stop at their office. We ordered there, and we had to go pick up our merchandise there, too. They never delivered."

"When I was a little girl, Robinson's Five and Ten was the place I shopped," Christina said. "They had everything that was small in size—needles, sunglasses, puzzles, dog collars, wrapping paper, swim flippers, picture frames, candles, and Fruit of the Loom underwear!"

"That store smelled heavenly," Janice added.

"I think it was the wooden floors. I miss those wooden floors."

"My favorite Christmas," Oscar said, "was when I was ten. Long before your time, little missy," he added, smiling at Wink. "I asked my parents for either a bike or a watch. Oh, they had money; they simply didn't believe in spending it. When I came down Christmas morning, there under the tree were a bike *and* a watch!"

"My favorite Christmas was when I got a Sparkle Plenty doll, like the girl in the Dick Tracy comics," Janice said. "She had braids coming out of the top of her head, and I could pull them to make them grow. Unfortunately, my brother pulled them too hard one day, and she ended up with two holes in her head. My mother knitted her a pretty pink hat with a flower on it."

"My favorite Christmas is *now*!" Wink said.

"I'll toast to that!" Andy said, holding out his wineglass.

Everyone at the table clinked glasses, even Wink, who had to kneel on her chair and lean forward enough to clink. Wink loved clinking glasses.

"Dessert is ice cream and Christmas cookies," Janice told them. "Tomorrow we'll have a special dessert, a baked Alaska." Turning to Wink, she said, "You can help me make it. And you can carry it in, if you promise to be careful. We're going to set it on fire."

Wink's eyes went round with wonder. "Oh, I'll be very careful!"

"Christina."

Oscar's voice still made Christina nervous. Weakly, she answered, "Yes?"

"We would like you to join us for Christmas dinner tomorrow."

"Oh, please please please!" Wink cried. "We really want you to come."

Christina hesitated. "I'm not sure . . ."

Delia spoke up. "Please join us, Christina." She sounded sincere.

"Yes, Christina," Andy said. "Please join us."

Christina took a deep breath. "I'd love to."

After dinner, everyone except Oscar carried plates and bowls into the kitchen. To Christina's surprise, Delia helped Janice load the dishwasher. Delia didn't look or act like someone who ever knew where the dishwasher was.

"We need to get home to get Wink to bed," Delia said.

"Yes, and I'll need to help Oscar," Janice added.

Andy looked at Christina. "Didn't you mention something about a midnight church service?"

Christina smiled. "Yes. It's at ten-thirty."

"I'd like to go with you," Andy said.

Of course you would, Christina thought, *because I've fallen and hit my head and all of this is a dream.*

"I'd love that," she answered.

It took a while for the others to gather their various boots, coats, and gloves. Christina and Andy stood on the porch, shivering in the cold, waving goodbye to Delia, Jeff, and Wink, who sat in the backseat of the Range Rover, and to Oscar and Janice, side by side in the front. Janice was driving. Wink, Christina saw through the window, was talking.

Christina and Andy sat together on the sofa, mugs of hot coffee in their hands, looking at the Christmas tree.

"Christina," Andy said, "I've decided to move here permanently. I've told my father."

"Wow," Christina said. "How did he take it?"

"He grumbled at first, but I discussed various ways I can branch off from investing into philanthropy. He's aware he's getting older, he's entertained by the idea of giving back, and the novelty of having people like him. He knows he'll stay here year-round."

"Does Janice have anything to do with this?"

Andy grinned. "Oh, yes. As you know, she grew up here and knows everything about the place. She took the job of cook and general housekeeper three years ago, and since then, well, with her help, Oscar has mellowed."

Christina muffled her IC who snipped, *If Oscar has mellowed I'm glad I didn't know him when he was tense!*

Andy continued, "I wouldn't be surprised if they had some kind of really leisurely romance going on. They developed a routine for their daily lives, revolving around meals, and Janice goes with him out to dinner or to movies or plays or to parties in the summer."

Christina smiled. "Lovely."

"Yes," Andy said, "being part of a couple is lovely for most people." He paused. He cleared his throat. He said, "I'd like to be part of a couple with you."

Christina couldn't believe what she'd just heard. She babbled on, as if what Andy had just said was something like *I'd like to believe a couple is two,* which didn't make any sense, but she was kind of in a state of shock.

"What about Wink? And Delia?"

"It's hard to believe but Delia and Jeff have reunited. Jeff flew to the island a few days ago and he and Delia spent some time together walking and talking on the beach. Jeff went back to the city, but he returned this morning. They've been acting like teenagers."

"What about Wink?" Christina asked.

"Delia thinks it will be best for Wink to have the security of the school and friends she's always had, so they haven't sold their city apartment. They'll return to the city after the holidays."

"Oh." Her heart dropped.

"Wink will spend part of the summer here, of course. And you and I could visit them when we go into the city. I'm willing to use Wink as a bargaining chip if it means you'll marry me."

So she wasn't hearing incorrectly. Now her heart flew to the top of her throat. She was becoming a one-person Cirque du Soleil. "Andy, we've only known each other for three weeks!"

"You've got to admit it's been a very special three weeks."

"True. Still. We should take time to get to know each other, don't you think? Remember, Andy, you were engaged to Anastasiya Belousova."

"True too. But I didn't love her, not like this. I was showing off. Livin' the dream. It was all an act to impress people. There was no real emotional connection."

Christina took a moment to reflect. She believed what Andy said. Andy had probably cared for Anastasiya once, but what she'd seen between Andy and the Russian model during the great water pipe disaster had been friendship, a neutral attachment.

"Okay," Christina said. "I get that. Still, this is all so hurried."

"I think it's been instantaneous. The Big Bang."

Christina blinked. That was what she'd always longed for. Slowly, she admitted, "My parents got married after they'd known each other a month. So I know it can happen."

Andy said, "Christina, *it's happening for us*." He paused. "And then, of course, there's this."

Leaning over, he took Christina in his arms and kissed her. Lightly at first, then with more warmth, and Christina felt every cell in her body responding to him, so that she kissed him back with passion. Soon they were half-lying on the sofa, their arms around each other, kissing as if they couldn't stop.

Breathless, Christina pulled away from him. They sat up, adjusting their clothes.

Andy grinned. "I think I can count on a definite maybe."

Christina looked into his eyes. She was thrilled and shaking with desire, and also terrified. "Yes, that's a definite maybe." She stood up, needing to move away from him before she fell on him, tore open his clothes and hers, and showed him it was really a blazing *YES*.

"Andy, it's almost ten-fifteen. The midnight service at St. Paul's starts at ten-thirty."

"Give me a minute to wash the lipstick off my face, and we'll go," Andy said.

St. Paul's Church on Fair Street looked a bit like a castle. Made out of pink granite and brownstone in a Romanesque style, it was decorated with several brilliant Tiffany stained glass windows. Inside, dark oak pews and carved pillars gave the church an air of mystery and grandeur, but in fact, it was a small church, holding only a few hundred. Fortunately, its members were bighearted, industrious, and talented. The church was gorgeously hung with green laurel and wreaths with grand red bows, and red poinsettias were set in the nooks that held the smaller stained glass windows.

Christina and Andy were just in time, but even so they had to squeeze into a pew at the back of the packed church. The rector, verger, and choir opened the service as they walked down the central aisle, singing "Hark! The Herald Angels Sing," and the congregation joined in. It was so beautiful Christina almost burst into tears. The service was mostly carols, and the choir was in splendid form, and Richard Loftin stood near the organ and embellished the music with the triumphant sounds from his trumpet.

Halfway through the service, Andy reached over and took Christina's hand in his.

"No," she whispered. "Not in church."

He smiled at her. "Yes. In church."

Afterward, Andy drove Christina home, walked her to her door, kissed her gently, and said good night.

21

Something about Christmas morning was magical. Christina lay in her bed for a while after she woke, not thinking, just taking in the day. The air seemed to glimmer and shine like a great light all around her.

She rose, pulled on her robe, and slid her feet into her slippers. The first thing she did when she got downstairs was to plug in the lights of the Christmas tree. She fed impatient Mittens, and made coffee.

She checked her cellphone. Several "Merry Christmas" messages from Mimi and other friends. A very loud MERRY CHRISTMAS from Wink. A quieter message from Andy, wishing her Merry Christmas and asking her to call when she was awake.

A selfie of Harriet and Jacob, both grinning joyfully. Jacob had lipstick all over his face. Harriet's lipstick was smeared.

Christina called Mimi. "Did you get Harriet and Jacob's kissy-face selfie?"

"I did." Mimi laughed.

"So Harriet wants to be with Jacob even if he's poor?"

"Oh, Christina, Jacob never said he was poor. He's privately very well-off. He's just one of those oddballs who wants to save the world. It's true, Harriet and Jacob are different, but you know the old saying that opposites attract." Mimi paused. "And how are you?"

"I'm happy and confused. Andy and his family surprised me last night when I got home. They'd made dinner and Christmas cookies, and we all got along famously."

"And . . . ?"

"And I'm going there this evening for dinner."

"And . . . ?"

"Oh, Mimi, Andy seems serious about me."

"*Serious?*"

"Well, he kind of proposed to me."

"Hot damn!" Mimi cried. "I'm not surprised. I could tell he was smitten the way he looked at you. What did you say?"

"I said *maybe*. Mimi, it's all too fast."

"I get that. And Christmas is so emotionally powerful, we all get caught up in the magic."

"So you think I should say no."

"What? NO! I mean, do not say no. I could see the way you looked at him, too. I've never seen you look like that at any man."

"Oh, Mimi, what shall I do?"

"Let your heart lead you," Mimi said.

Listen to her, her Inner Christina said. *She's right. Or you can listen to me 'cause I'll say the same thing and I* won't *politely shut up.*

"You're so bossy," Christina told herself.

"I don't mean to be bossy," Mimi said. "You asked—"

"No, no, Mimi, I didn't mean you!" Christina thought fast. "I mean that, um, *Mittens* is bossy. She's always whapping her tail against my legs. She wants more food. I'd better feed her. And, Mimi, thank you for the advice."

"You're welcome. Merry Christmas, Christina!"

Some Christmas cookies had been left for her, so Christina ate a reindeer, a snowman, and a star for her breakfast. She lounged on the sofa as she talked on the phone, to Louise and to Dora, who had gotten an American Girl doll from Santa and wanted to describe every accessory. To Wink, who was bursting with the news that Santa had given her a makeup kit AND a sparkly slime-making kit. To Georgina Smithers, who had been one of Christina's mother's best friends.

And to Harriet and Jacob, who quite obviously had spent the night together.

"Isn't this wonderful, Christina?" Harriet asked. She'd secluded herself in the bathroom of her apartment so she could whisper in privacy.

"It is wonderful. And totally surprising."

"We're taking time to get to know each other," Harriet said. "I hope this ends up happily ever after, but right now, I'm just happy to enjoy the day."

"That's wise of you, Harriet," Christina said.

"It is, isn't it? Who would have thought!"

When her phone calls tapered off, Christina dressed

quickly and hurried down to her store to choose presents for Andy, Wink, and the others. Back home, she wrapped them all and tucked them into a book bag.

Relaxing at last, Christina took a long, hot shower and washed her hair, and rubbed cream into her skin, and blew her hair dry. She slipped into her favorite robe and lay on the sofa, reading a book her parents had bought her for Christmas. Actually, she had bought it, but Mimi had suggested after her parents died that she keep their memory alive by buying herself a present she knew they would give her. She read Patti Callahan's *Becoming Mrs. Lewis*, about the woman who married C. S. Lewis. Later, she put a bookmark in the book and turned on her television and searched for *The Chronicles of Narnia*. She loved the lion.

She wondered if Wink had seen this movie or heard of the book.

Finally it was time to go to Oscar's house for Christmas dinner. She wore her knee-high red leather boots—which had recovered nicely from the water-pipe incident, just as Harriet promised—her red silk dress, and earrings shaped like tree lights that blinked on and off. Today was Christmas, and she felt festive. She redid her cherry red lipstick, picked up her bag of presents, and drove to Oscar's house.

22

Wink threw the door open the moment Christina pulled into the driveway.

"You're here! Finally!" Wink was so excited, she jumped up and down as she talked. "We have presents for you!"

Delia appeared behind her daughter. "Sweetie, you're letting cold air into the house. Let Christina get inside before you start chattering at her."

Christina stepped inside—it was wonderfully warm— and bent to kiss Wink. From the kitchen came the aroma of delicious baking.

"What's in the bag?" Wink asked.

"Presents for everyone, of course," Christina told her.

Andy appeared. "Let me take your coat."

The sight of Andy and Delia together made Christina blink. "Um, you're wearing Christmas sweaters."

"Yes, we are." Delia bugged out her eyes and smiled determinedly. "Wink gave us each a sweater for Christmas."

"Grandfather helped me buy them," Wink said. "Aren't they cool?"

Both sweaters were gaudily embellished with Christmas themes. Delia had a smiling white-haired Mrs. Santa Claus in the kitchen with the elves stirring a steaming pot. Andy wore a reindeer with antlers and a bright red nose.

"They are extremely cool," Christina agreed.

"Merry Christmas, Christina," Delia's husband said. The front of his sweater dazzled with an enormous and extremely decorated Christmas tree.

"Merry Christmas, Jeff," Christina said. "Wow, you have a Christmas sweater, too!"

"I got Daddy one," Wink cried, "because I didn't want him to be left out at Christmas! And wait till you see what I got for you!" Wink took Christina's hand and pulled her toward the living room.

Seated in the large leather chair by the crackling fire was Oscar. He also wore a Christmas sweater. His was decorated with a stag with candelabras of antlers standing proudly on a mountain. Appropriate, Christina thought, Oscar *was* the leader of the herd.

Her Inner Christina cheered: *Mimi must have been thrilled to sell so many sweaters!*

"Sit here, next to me!" Wink invited, patting a sofa cushion.

Christina sat, cradling her book bag in her lap. "I brought presents for everyone."

"Wait!" Wink cried. "You have to open your present from me first!"

"Don't be bossy," Delia told her daughter. Turning to Christina, she said, "But yes, you really should open your present first."

"I'll get it!" Wink scrambled to the floor, took a large present from under the tree, and handed it to Christina.

It was a Christmas sweater. Penguins and polar bears wearing Santa hats danced over the crimson acrylic between snowflakes sparkling with sequins.

"Thank you, Wink!"

"Put it on, Christina!"

Christina slid the sweater over her head. It was loose, and the neckline was itchy, but she declared that she loved it and would wear it every Christmas. Wink glowed with pride.

"Hello, everyone." Janice came into the room, carrying a tray of drinks. "Champagne for the grown-ups, pink 7Up for Miss Wink."

Andy jumped up. "Let me help you with that."

"I see you got your Christmas sweater," Janice said with a grin.

"Yes," Christina said, modeling it for her. "I see you got yours, too."

"I wore it this morning when I had Christmas with my mother and daughters," Janice said. "My girls made the Christmas dinner and it was like old times. Tonight I'm getting my second Christmas."

Janice's sweater was a stunning purple embroidered with Christmas packages, each package tied with bows of green, red, and blue. Looking at it, Christina was extremely thankful she wasn't hungover. Janice winked at Christina and left the room.

"May I give out my presents now?" Christina asked Wink, who seemed to be the master of ceremonies this evening.

Wink was wriggling with excitement. "Sure!"

"Why don't I hand them to you, Wink, and you can be my elf and deliver them."

"Yay!"

Delia got an enormous jigsaw puzzle of the island. "Wink, you can help me with this!"

Oscar's present was a game of Nantucketopoly, with a board like Monopoly, but each bit of real estate a business on Nantucket. Christina's toy store wasn't featured, nor were any of the sheds—they were too insignificant.

Wink received the gorgeous book about the mermaid. "Thank you, Christina!" She threw her arms around Christina and hugged her.

"Here, Wink. This is for your father." Christina held out an extremely small present wrapped with a large bow. It was only a pack of cards backed with a map of Nantucket, but she thought Jeff would understand.

"This is great!" Jeff said when he opened his present. "Wink, I'm going to teach you how to play gin rummy."

"And I'll teach you how to play crazy eights!" Wink said.

"Thank you, Christina," Jeff said.

"You're welcome," Christina replied. "Here, Wink. Take this last present to your uncle."

Andy seemed puzzled when he opened it. "A bag of marbles?"

To everyone's surprise, Oscar spoke up. "You've never played marbles? I'll have to teach you."

"And me, too, Grandfather!" Wink said.

Delia rose and came toward Christina, which was slightly unnerving.

"Andy tells me you're a bit prickly about receiving presents, so I stuck with the tried and true. This is from all of us."

Christina tidily undid the wrapping paper to find a bottle of Joy perfume. "Thank you, everyone."

"Now let's go eat!" Wink cried.

"Wait, Wink. I've got another present for Christina."

Andy crossed the room and sat next to Christina. He handed her his present.

Christina peeled away the silver paper to find a small black velvet box. She hesitated before opening it. When she opened it, she gasped. The ring was a beautiful ruby surrounded by diamonds.

She knew her face was flushing as she gazed at the ring.

"I'd like to think of it as a pre-engagement ring," Andy said softly.

"It belonged to my mother," Oscar announced, a catch in his voice.

"It belonged to Oscar's mother?" Christina was dumbfounded. It was true that during this hour in the Bittlesmans' house, she felt welcome and happy and among friends. It was true that she loved Andy. But wait! Her mind was racing. She tried to slow herself down. "This is an amazing gift, Andy." She looked into his blue eyes and what she saw there warmed her to the bottom of her heart. "But it's an *heirloom*. I don't know—"

"Oh, Christina," Wink said, "just take it!"

Christina laughed. "Okay. I will."

Andy took the ring from its velvet nest and slid it onto Christina's finger.

It fit perfectly.

Christina burst into tears.

"Mommy, why is Christina crying?" Wink asked, alarmed.

"Sometimes people cry when they're happy," Delia told her.

Andy took Christina in his arms. He whispered in her ear, "I love you."

Janice said, "Wink, she's probably crying because she's hungry. I think we should have dinner." She hurried out of the room.

Oscar rose from his chair. "Come on, Wink, let's lead everyone into dinner."

Wink seized her grandfather's hand. "It's like a parade!"

After Wink and Oscar came Delia and Jeff, then Christina and Andy. They processed into the dining room. Christina gasped. Janice was lighting candles that stood among a king's ransom of silver gleaming on the long table. The centerpiece was a long, low, lush mix of red and white roses. Sparkling crystal glasses and silver flatware sat close to white and red china.

Oscar announced that Janice had cooked the food but

he had hired several people from a catering staff to help her serve. The room echoed with laughter as they enjoyed the tender roast lamb, buttered vegetables, and wine, and for Wink, bubbling water. When Wink carried in the flaming baked Alaska, everyone clapped and Wink's face was rosy with joy. A server poured champagne, and Jeff let his daughter taste a sip, and Christina saw how Delia's face softened as she watched her husband with their little girl.

When the meal finished, Oscar rose. "And now it's time for my traditional Christmas nap."

"What a good idea," Delia said. "Wink, let's go upstairs. Daddy and I are going to take a nap. You may read or play with your toys, but we're all going to rest. You'll stay in your room for an hour."

"I'll carry you up," Jeff said, and lifted a delighted Wink onto his shoulders.

Christina and Andy returned to the living room and stood a moment looking at the tall, glorious tree.

"What would you like to do now?" Andy asked.

"Truly? I'd like to be in my own house with you. It's silly, but I haven't given Mittens her present yet, and . . ."

"And it's more private," Andy finished for her.

"Yes." Christina grinned. "There is that."

"I'll get my keys," Andy said, moving toward the hall.

"Or not," Christina said. "You could ride over with me." She paused. "And spend the night."

"I can't think of anything I'd like more," Andy told her.

They shrugged into their warm coats and caps and gloves and hurried out to her car. The town was quiet as if hushed by the snowy day. Christina had left her Christmas tree lights on, and when she pulled into the driveway, she saw Mittens sitting in the window, looking forlorn. They hurried into her house and shed their coats.

"Poor lonely girl," Christina said, picking up the cat and cuddling her.

She curled up on the sofa into Andy's arms, and the cat snuggled up to Christina.

"This is the perfect way to get warm," she said. Lifting her hand, she turned it this way and that, watching the gems sparkle in the light. "Andy, this is a beautiful gift."

"The first of many, I hope." He shifted on the sofa, pulling a cushion behind him. "I'm planning to move here in January. I've told Oscar I'd like to live with him for a few months to get used to island life in the winter and to let you get used to the thought of marriage."

Christina nodded and stroked her fingers through Mittens's fur. The cat purred.

"Andy, is there any chance that if, when, we get married, we could live in this house? It's a solid house, and it's large and roomy and close to town . . ."

"I don't know, Christina," Andy said. "It's a possibility. But you know, I've never seen the second floor of this house."

"Oh, it's wonderful," Christina assured him. "Five bedrooms, only one bath, but there's a fireplace in the master bedroom."

"Could you show me?" Andy asked with a gleam in his eye.

"Of course," Christina said. "Let's go up—"

Someone pounded loudly on the front door. Mittens leapt from Christina's arms and hid under the sofa.

Christina straightened her clothing and went to the door, feeling worried and miffed by the interruption.

"Christina!" Mimi cried.

"Christina!" Harriet cried.

"Christina!" Jacob cried.

The three crowded in to her front hall.

"Is everything okay?" Andy came to stand by her, his hand on her waist, and she was grateful for the comfort. *What now?* her Inner Christina demanded.

"Look!" Jacob said. Pulling an envelope out of his pocket, he said, "Delia came to my house this afternoon."

"Delia came to your house?" Christina asked.

"She said her father asked her to deliver this letter to me, and I was to share it with all of you, and you all would get your own letter in the mail."

"Have you read it yet?" Mimi asked.

"I've been tempted, but I waited for you all. I'll open it and read it now, all right?"

Christina, Harriet, and Mimi nodded.

Jacob began to read. "'To Mimi Mattes, Jacob Greenwood, Harriet—'"

"Jacob!" Harriet cried. "Cut to the chase!"

"'Because of the one absorbing hour I spent in Christina's Toy Shop, I decided that . . .' Oh, my gosh!" Jacob was shocked into silence.

"Jacob!" Harriet yelled.

"Sorry, sorry. It's just such a surprise. Here we go, '. . . I decided that the buildings on the wharf are uncomfortable, cramped, and bitterly cold in the winter and unsuitable for such talented people as you four. Therefore I have ordered my lawyer to draw up papers to lower the rent paid on these buildings by twenty percent.'"

"Shut up!" Harriet cried. Leaning forward, she pulled the letter from Jacob's hand. "Get out of town! That's really what it says. Twenty percent!" She handed the letter to Mimi. She threw her arms around Christina. "You did it! Thank you! Oh, where's the champagne? We should celebrate!"

"There's more," Mimi said, staring at the letter.

"What?" Harriet cried.

"'If Christina Antonioni tries to talk you out of this, don't let her. She does not receive gifts easily. Furthermore, this is not a personal gift. This is a business decision.'"

Harriet, Jacob, and Mimi stared at Christina.

"I will kill you with my bare hands," Harriet threatened.

"You won't have to," Christina promised. "I'm delighted with this letter."

She looked up at Andy. "Did you know about this?"

"Not the specifics, but the general idea," Andy said.

"It's only logical," Christina said. "Because Oscar managed to stay in the shed for an hour, he learned the condition the sheds are in."

"*Oscar,* is it now?" Harried asked, arching one eyebrow.

"Yes. It's Oscar." Christina had to bite her tongue to keep from boasting, *He's going to be my father-in-law.* Harriet would have to be revived with brandy if she knew that.

"This is a spectacular Christmas present!" Mimi said.

"But this isn't all because of my challenge," Christina reminded them. "What does it say in the letter? The sheds are unsuitable for such talented people as we four? I'd say that's quite a compliment to our caroling!"

"Maybe you're right," Harriet said.

"Well, I think it's wonderful," Andy told them all. "I'm sure my father was touched by the caroling, and I'm also sure that once he knew the state of the sheds, he knew he should live up to his responsibilities as a landlord and improve your buildings."

"I agree," Jacob said.

As if she'd only just noticed it, Harriet said, "Oh, you're here, Andy. I mean on Christmas Day." Cattily, she added, "How nice for Christina not to have to be alone."

And then, because it was true, and wonderful, and because she was only human after all, Christina said, "I'm not sure 'nice' does justice to the occasion." And she flashed her ruby and diamond ring.

Harriet shrieked. Mimi hugged her. Jacob said, "Congratulations."

Mimi, always the most sensitive one, said, "Okay, we're leaving now!"

"But, the champagne," Harriet said.

"We'll have it at my house." Mimi politely redistributed her bulk so that she could urge Harriet and Jacob to the door. "Merry Christmas!"

Christina and Andy stood in the doorway waving good-bye to their unexpected guests.

"What a great Christmas present," Christina said.

"I think you were just about to show me the upstairs of the house," Andy reminded her with a smile.

"So you'd really like to live here when we"—*Don't freeze now,* her Inner Christina commanded—"are married?"

"Yeah," Andy answered. "I like this house."

"I like you in it."

Christina took his hand as they went up the stairs.

They didn't come down until morning.

about the author

NANCY THAYER is the *New York Times* best-selling author of more than thirty novels, including *Surfside Sisters*, *A Nantucket Wedding*, *Secrets in Summer*, *The Island House*, *The Guest Cottage*, *An Island Christmas*, *Nantucket Sisters*, and *Island Girls*. Born in Kansas, Thayer has been a resident of Nantucket for thirty-five years, where she currently lives with her husband, Charley, and a precocious rescue cat named Callie.

nancythayer.com

Facebook.com/NancyThayerBooks

about the type

This book was set in Fairfield, the first type-face from the hand of the distinguished American artist and engraver Rudolph Ruzicka (l883–1978). Ruzicka was born in Bohemia (in the present-day Czech Republic) and came to America in 1894. He set up his own shop, devoted to wood engraving and printing, in New York in 1913 after a varied career working as a wood engraver, in photoengraving and banknote printing plants, and as an art director and freelance artist. He designed and illustrated many books, and was the creator of a considerable list of individual prints— wood engravings, line engravings on copper, and aquatints.